# DOING TIME IN HELL

# DOING TIME IN HELL

A Story of Love,
Loyalty, Betrayal,
Greed, and Denial

MISTER 1610

**To order additional copies of this book, contact:**
Xlibris
1-888-795-4274
www.Xlibris.com
Orders@Xlibris.com
806669

*In memory of:*

*Robert Rainey*
*Sue Moorer*
*Maurice White*
*Anthony White*
*Jerry White*
*Tiny-Loc*
*Danny Ray Bartley*
*LaZette "Boo" Bolen*

*Gone from earth, but not forgotten.*

# PREFACE

Cdog heard a knock on the door but knew who it was
before the knock came because he was looking out the window once he heard
the loud music. It was Big Cdog, the nigga he was named after and the nigga
who was fucking his sister, Karen.

"What it do, lil homie?" asked Big Cdog when Lil Cdog opened the door.

"It ain't shit, my nigga," came the reply.

"Where my girl at?" Big Cdog asked.

"That rat upstairs," Lil Cdog said, laughing.

"Get off my girl, lil nigga," said Big Cdog, and bust out laughing also.

"Ayee, trip, that nigga Tank sent that tramp-ass bitch Lisa over here,
talking about he need a package and a few dollars on his books," said Lil
Cdog.

"Oh yeah, is that nigga still in the same spot?" asked Big Cdog, referring
to the prison Tank was in.

"Yeah, he still there," said Lil Cdog.

"So did you hook him up?" asked Big Cdog.

"After I finish slamming my dick down her throat, I gave her a few dollars
for the nigga," said Lil Cdog, and they both laughed.

"Stay away from that bitch. She poison," Big Cdog said in a serious tone.
"She doing the same shit she did to Junebug."

"But Tank's dumb ass made her his girl. We both was fucking the bitch
back then when Junebug first went to jail," said Lil Cdog.

"I'm telling you, every nigga that fuck with her end up in jail, so just be
careful, lil homie."

"I got you, my nigga," stated Lil Cdog.

"What's all the loud laughing for in my house?" asked Karen.

"We just shooting the shit," said Big Cdog as he grabbed her ass then pulled her toward him.

"Y'all need to get a room for all that shit," said Lil Cdog, smiling.

"Naw, nigga. You need to figure out what college you going to. Then we would have a room," said Karen.

"Now you sounding like Momma," Lil Cdog replied.

"She right though, nigga," Big Cdog added.

"Yeah, yeah, yeah," said Lil Cdog, now becoming irritated.

"Let's get up outta here before the little nigga kill up the house," Big Cdog said, which made them all laugh.

"Don't have none of those tramps in here while I'm gone," said Karen.

"They ain't no trampier than your ass," Lil Cdog said, laughing.

"Fuck you, nigga," Karen said, getting a little mad.

"Don't dish it out if you can't take it," said Lil Cdog.

"Whateva. You heard what I said," Karen stated as she and Big Cdog walked out of the front door.

"Don't forget about that business we need to handle later," Big Cdog said over his shoulder.

"I won't, my nigga," replied Lil Cdog.

"Don't get my little brother in no trouble," said Karen, frowning at Big Cdog.

"Shut that shit up," came Big Cdog's reply as he dug his fingers in her ass.

Now that Cdog was alone, he sat down on the couch to think, and what his sister had said about school went thru his mind.

"Yeah, I gotta start making some real decisions about my future," he said out loud to himself. "I know once Mom and Pop get back from their vacation, I'll have to hear the same shit from them," Cdog mumbled, followed by a sigh.

He got up, grabbed his keys, and headed toward the door.

*** Two hours later, on the block, Lil Cdog was bent down at the dice game.

"Bet I hit for this dove," he said.

"Bet you don't, nigga," said Popeye.

"Hit dice," said Cdog, and then he rolled them out.

"Snake eyes!" Popeye yelled as he snatched his money off the ground.

The whole dice game looked up to see a car pulling up, bumping music so loud, no one could hear each other. It was Big Cdog. Popeye glanced at Hotdog, his brother, but Hotdog was so drunk, he didn't even look his brother's way. Big Cdog walked up to the dice game and smiled when his eyes fell on Hotdog. *I finally caught this nigga*, Big Cdog thought to himself.

"What's up, Cdog?" Popeye asked nervously, but because of the music, Cdog didn't hear him.

Big Cdog tapped Lil Cdog on the shoulder and motioned for him to check it out. They walked toward the car, and the dice game watched as they jumped in, with Big Cdog in the driver's seat.

"Damn, that was close," mumbled Popeye. *I gotta get this nigga outta here as soon as Cdog pull off*, thought Popeye.

The music seemed to get louder as the car begin to pull off. The car suddenly came to a stop, with the dice game looking at the passenger-side door. Popeye wouldn't had known shots were coming from the car had he not been shot in the arm. He yelled out to his brother, but the music was just too fucking loud.

Inside the car, Big Cdog had the seventeen-shot Glock in his hand, aimed at Hotdog. Lil Cdog had his seat leaned back so he would be out of the line of fire, but to those at the dice game, the shots appeared to come from the passenger seat. Big Cdog let off ten to twelve shots so quickly, no one had time to react. When Cdog emptied the clip, he put the car in gear and drove off, already knowing he got his man.

Now that the music was gone, the dice game could hear each other. Most were yelling, and others were groaning from being shot. Popeye looked toward his brother and saw the hole in his head before he saw the brain splattered.

"That nigga killed my brother!" shouted Popeye. "That bitch-ass nigga Lil Cdog killed my brother!" yelled Popeye once more before he broke down crying.

\*\*\* Eleven months after Hotdog was killed, Lil Cdog was on his way to doing life in hell.

# DOING LIFE IN HELL

## A Story of Love, Loyalty, Betrayal, Greed, and Denial

# Cdog, Tank, and Junebug

*How the hell did I allow Big Cdog to put me here?*
Lil Cdog asked himself as he lay on his bunk, wide awake at three in the morning.

"Bottom bunk, don't you move!" yelled a correctional officer (a.k.a. c/o).

"Top bunk, step down and back up towards the door with your hands up!" yelled another c/o.

"Man, why ya'll fucking with us? We ain't done shit!" the guy from the top bunk screamed as he backed toward the door.

"Shut up and keep coming back!" yelled the officer.

"What you mean shut up?" asked the top-bunk guy as he began to spin around on the officers.

"Get down! Get down on the floor!" was all Cdog can hear being yelled by numerous c/os mixed with the sound of the alarm one of them had pushed. Then came the sound of Mace being sprayed.

"What the fuck, man? I can't breathe. Why you spray me?" the guy from the top bunk asked.

"Get your ass on the floor!" screamed a c/o before the sound of someone's body being slammed on concrete came.

It was supposed to be one of their surprise searches, but the whole building was now awake and coughing from the smell of Mace. *It is 3:00 a.m., and the army got the nerve to say they do more before 6:00 a.m. than most people do all day*, Cdog thought with a smile.

1

"Yard tower, be advised. We have two 10-15s being escorted to medical," said a c/o into the walkie-talkie.

Cdog stood at the cell door and watched as his neighbor was being taken away. "Oh, well. I'm up now, so let me make a shot of coffee and wait for breakfast," Cdog said out loud to himself.

\*\*\* Three hours later at the chow hall table, the conversation was about the raid.

"Man, I think they used like five cans of spray on them fools," said Junebug.

"I'm tired of how these bitch-ass police get at us," Cdog said.

"I think they need another demo like that last prison, when dudes ran in the program office on their ass," said Tank.

"Shit, I'm ready to go."

Just like that, a plan of retaliation was formed.

"Let's wait and see if they bring them cats back," said Junebug.

"Shit, that ain't nothing but an excuse not to do something," Tank said while mad-dogging Junebug.

"Nigga, I'm ready wheneva," shot Junebug.

*I wonder if he mean ready to do it with the police or do it with Tank*, thought Cdog to himself then said "Look, homie, this ain't the time or place for ya'll to go at it with each other. We on some other shit," Cdog said to Junebug and Tank.

"Yeah, alrite, my nigga," Junebug said to Cdog, but he was thinking about how he couldn't wait to put his knife in Tank. *Shit, I might even put my dick in him too*, he thought with a smile. *These niggas come to jail. Then we all homies, but when the nigga was out, he was fucking my bitch. Wouldn't even tell the bitch to bring my daughter to visit me. Yeah, I'll leave it alone for now, but I won't forget, nigga.*

"Snap out of it, my boy," Cdog said to Junebug. "They called our table to leave."

"My bad. I was straight somewhere else," said Junebug.

"You right, homie. Let's wait and see if they bring those dudes back," said Tank to Junebug.

"Whateva," said Junebug as he walked off.

"Y'all need to resolve ya'll situation," Cdog said to Tank now that they were alone.

"Shit, it ain't my fault he fell in love with a rat," Tank said with a smile, which made Cdog smile, also because just like Tank, he too was running up in Junebug's bitch before he had come to jail.

"Yeah, she is a rat," said Cdog. "But as homies, we don't need to be in here going at it with each other. Shit, prison politics got us apart of a car, but in reality, it's me, you, and Junebug against the yard, and that's a thousand muthafuckas." said Cdog.

"Don't trip. I'll holla at him, but I'm not kissing no ass except for his baby momma ass," Tank said, which made them both laugh out loud.

"I'll catch you when they open up the yard," said Cdog.

"Fo' sho', my nigga," Tank said as they shook hands.

Cdog had just finished cleaning his cell when they announced over the intercom, "Five minutes 'til yard."

Cdog got his stuff together and waited. Out on the yard, everyone was at their respective table or area, with the morning raid being the key topic, until a homie came up and said, "The Mexicans supposed to lay the yard down, so if you dirty, get it off you."

"Oh yeah, they about to book Smiley for all the bullshit he been in," said Tank.

"Damn, that fool owe me a few dollars," said Insane, a nigga off the east side.

"You can chalk that up," Cdog said. "Let me go put this up before this shit go down."

"I'll walk with you," Tank said.

After burying the two knives, Cdog asked, "Where's Junebug?"

"That fool had a phone call," said Tank.

"Look, there they go," Cdog said to Tank as two Mexicans walked up to Smiley and began stabbing him.

"They getting his ass good," said Tank.

"I know, and the police haven't seen shit yet," said Cdog.

"Man, they might kill him," stated Tank in an excited voice.

"No shit. They already stab him over twenty times," said Cdog.

"Get down! Everybody get down on the yard!" yelled the tower officer as he cocked the Mini-14 rifle.

"Get off him now!" yelled the c/os.

"Two on one, weapons involved," said a c/o into his walkie-talkie.

"Stand back!" ordered the sergeant to the c/os. "All towers, take your shot if you have it!" barked the sergeant into his walkie-talkie. "This your final warning. Get off him, or you will be shot," said the sergeant, which seemed to trigger a barrage of shots from two of the six towers.

"They shot him in the back," said Tank.

"I see that shit," Cdog said.

"Hold all fire!" barked the sergeant into his walkie-talkie. "Be advised. We have three inmates down. Medical transport is needed," he continued on the walkie-talkie.

"These Mexicans will be on lockdown for a while for this," said Tank.

"Hell yeah, they will. Shit, I think Smiley may be dead," Cdog said.

"Him and that one fool they shot," said Tank.

"Man, welcome to life in hell. I bet Junebug happy he stayed in for his call. Nigga, we about to be out here on the ground for a while, and you know they going to strip-search everybody," said Cdog.

"Man, look at all that blood," said Tank.

"Be advised. Silent alarm in Building 4," the c/o's walkie-talkie said.

"Gotta be a false alarm," stated Tank as the sergeant only told three c/os to respond to the building.

"Staff assault able. Side dayroom. One 10-15," said a c/o over the walkie-talkie.

Four to five c/os ran toward the building, and when the side door opened, the inmates on the yard could hear the bloc gun being fired.

Cdog and Tank looked at each other and asked the same question: "Staff assault?"

"Whoeva it is, they doing their shit because they still shooting," said Tank.

"Look, nigga, they just lifted the Mexican they shot onto the stretcher, and I swear, his guts fell out," said Cdog.

"Damn. This been an active-ass day, and it all started with that raid," Tank said.

"I just seen a medical van pull up to the back of Building 4," said Cdog.

"They trying to sneak whoeva that is outta here," replied Tank.

"Smiley must be dead because they took the other two Mexicans already, but they still got him laid out," Cdog said.

"And look, they ain't striping nobody and then just want us off the yard," said Tank.

"Yeah, I see," said Cdog. Then he added, "I'll holla when they let us back out. I'm sure it will be at least two weeks for everybody except the Mexicans."

"We will see, homie. Peace," replied Tank.

"Peace," said Cdog.

Cdog wasn't back in his cell ten minutes when he heard someone yelling his name in the vent.

"Hey, Cdog!" the voice yelled.

"What it do?" asked Cdog.

"Top of the day to you. This Rosco. Aye, you know that was your homie Junebug in here getting down with the police, right?"

"Naw, I didn't know that. They took him out the back door, so we never saw who it was," answered Cdog.

"Yeah, he came to my door when he heard the alarm on the yard and said it was ya'll against the police, so he took off on the floor cop," said Rosco.

All Cdog could do was shake his head at the vent. "That was them Mexicans out there cleaning up their shit, but good looking on the info, homie. You have a solid day," said Cdog. *Damn*, Cdog was thinking as he sat down on the bunk. *If we had known that was the homie, we would've never came back to our cells.* "Don't trip, Junebug. We on our way," Cdog said out loud to himself with a smile on his face. *Let me strike Tank a kite and have it ready when they cell-feed us*, thought Cdog.

> *Top of the day, homie. Aye, I don't know if you heard, but that was Junebug in here fighting the pigs. The boy Rosco said he thought that was us out there, so he took off. Now we both know what we gotta do once these doors open. Have a good day. Ima holla later.*
>
> *w/r,*
>
> *Cdog*

*Man, this some bullshit*, thought Tank after he finished reading Cdog's kite. *What the fuck he mean we know what we gotta do? Nigga, you don't run shit. Junebug's stupid ass brought this on himself. He so wrapped up on that bitch, he can't think straight.* "Yeah, Cdog, you right. I do know what I gotta do," Tank said out loud to himself. "I do know what I gotta do."

\*\*\* *Damn, my head ain't never hurt this bad in my life*, thought Junebug, *and every time I breathe in, it hurt. That fool in the tower shot me like six times with that bloc gun, and niggas always say that muthafucka don't hurt. I did get my man though.* He thought and tried to smile, but his lips also hurt.

*Man, once they put me in that medical van, they took turns whipping my ass all the way to the hospital. I should be here for a while. I hope I can get word to my mom. Naw, fuck that.* Junebug thought, *Word to my baby momma. Once she hear about my situation, she will come running, and everything will be all right. I'll forgive her for her fuck-ups, but Ima still get that nigga Tank,* Junebug thought and once again tried to smile. *I know when I leave here, I'll be going to the hole and then off to do a SHU program, but I'll see you again, Tank. We got unfinished business, nigga.*

That was Junebug's last thought before the medication put him to sleep.

"Johnson, what's your last two?" a c/o asked, standing at Cdog's door.

"Seven one," Cdog replied, referring to the last two digits of his prison number.

"You got legal mail. Sign next to your name," the c/o said.

*Let me see what these people gotta say now. They know they screwed up on my case but just don't wanna take this time off me,* Cdog thought.

> The State of Texas v. Curtis Johnson hereby request the court to grant another month for our response to plaintiff's petition.

"Straight bullshit," Cdog said out loud. "They know how to put a nigga in here with no delays but delay the fuck outta letting a nigga go." *Man, I need to use the phone,* he thought. *It's already been three weeks since we went on lockdown. Only the whites and the others got program. They claim the blacks may come off soon because they believe the attack by Junebug was isolated. Hold up. Now that I think about it, that nigga Tank never replied to my kite. He better be ready when we do come off,* thought Cdog.

*** *Man, I been back here in the hole for three weeks now and still haven't got my write-up,* thought Junebug. *And then to add more bullshit on top of bullshit, since leaving the hospital, I come to find out that was the Mexicans out on the yard getting that fool Smiley. Shit had nothing to do with us, but that's cool. Can't cry over spilled milk. What ain't cool is how my baby momma not once came to the hospital to check on me, and I know for sure that nurse called because she said a girl name Nesha answered the phone. That's my sister-in-law, and I know she gave Lisa the message. I'll just write her and my daughter a letter and let them know I'm all right,* thought Junebug to himself.

*** *Man, I can't let these niggas fuck mine off,* Tank thought. *They don't know, but my shit was overturned like ten months ago. Now I'm supposed to catch an assault on the police and get a three-strike sentence for that dumbass nigga Junebug? I can't wait to get out and stick my dick in his baby momma mouth again.* Tank grabbed his dick. "Ima send your ass some photos this time," Tank said out loud with a smile on his face. *I got something for all you niggas, especially you, Cdog. Naw, I don't love Lisa, and she wasn't my main bitch, but that nigga knew I was fucking her when he decided to push up on her. Now the nigga in here in mine, and Junebug's face acting like she ain't done shit. Fuck both of ya'll in my eyes,* thought Tank. *Ima just kick back and let this plan unfold.*

"Do you want a shower?" a c/o asked Tank, appearing out of nowhere.

"Yeah, I do," Tank answered.

"Shower shoes and boxers only. Put your hands thru the tray slot to be handcuffed," the c/o said.

"Aye, how long this shit gon' last?" asked Tank.

"I would say two, maybe three more weeks, but you never know around here," replied the c/o.

"Damn," said Tank as he got in the shower. "I thought they said it was an isolated incident?" Tank asked the c/o.

"They still investigating," said the c/o as he walked off.

*Boom, boom, boom, boom* was the sound on the wall in Cdog's cell as Tank knocked.

"Yo, what's up?" asked Cdog.

"This Tank, nigga," came the reply.

"Damn, homie. I was just thinking about you and was going to holla down there after dinner," said Cdog.

"That's right, my nigga. Aye, my bad on not responding to your kite," shot Tank.

"Don't trip, but you felt what I was saying, right?" asked Cdog.

"One hundred percent, I did. It is what it is. You feel me?" said Tank.

"Yes, sir, I do. I'm just tying up any loose ends I may have before the doors open," said Cdog.

"That's what's up, my nigga," Tank stated.

"I got another letter from the DA asking the court for more time," said Cdog. Then he asked, "Have you heard anything on your shit?"

"Naw, I haven't," lied Tank. "I'm playing the waiting game."

"Damn, nigga. You put your appeal in over four years ago, right?" Cdog asked with suspicion in his voice.

"Sometime they fast. Sometime they slow. I'm not tripping." Tank continued his lie. "Aye, here come the pigs to take me back to my cell. If you need something, just holla," said Tank.

"Likewise, my boy. Enjoy the rest of your day," said Cdog as he sat back down on his bunk. *Something ain't right with that nigga*, thought Cdog, *but I just can't put my finger on it. He better show up when these doors open though.*

\*\*\* *Man, it's been two weeks since I wrote Lisa and still no reply*, thought Junebug. *She must not be getting my mail. I bet these bitch-ass police throwing my shit in the trash*, Junebug said to himself—any excuse to ease his mind of the reality that Lisa really didn't give a fuck about him anymore. "Then these muthafuckas wanna give me a thirty-six-month SHU on top of beating my ass," Junebug said out loud. *One day, all ya'll will pay for how ya'll treating the bug*, he thought. "Let me get my ass up and burn away some of this stress," Junebug said out loud. "Fuck everybody in the world except for Lisa and my daughter!" he screamed out loud, enough for the next three cells to hear him.

\*\*\* "Who the fuck that nigga Cdog think he is?" Tank asked himself. "Who made him Frank White of this shit?" *Then the nigga got the nerve to ask me about my appeal. My business is my business.* "Just watch my black ass walk outta here, nigga, while you do the rest of your life in this bitch," Tank said in a whisper so his neighbors couldn't hear him. *I can't wait until we come off lockdown for this shit to unfold*, Tank thought to himself. "I will get the last laugh, nigga" he said out loud with a smile.

\*\*\* *Look like we almost done with this lockdown*, Cdog thought as he stood at his cell door. *They starting their interviews, so it won't be long now. They already searched three of the five buildings. My block should be next, but they may make us last since this the building everything started from. Yeah, they might hit us hard, but that's if though*, Cdog thought with a smile. *We gon' hit ya'll ass harder when this door open.*

Suddenly, the lyrics of the Notorious B.I.G. came to his mind, and Cdog started snapping his fingers in tune as the words begin to leave his lips.

"Somebody got to die. If I go, you gotta go. Ha ha ha ha!" Cdog laughed out loud. *That nigga couldn't had said it any better.*

*** "Do you want yard?" the c/o asked, standing at Junebug's cell.

"Naw, I'm cool," replied Junebug. *Them muthafuckas know damn well I haven't been to their kettle cage since I been back here, so why keep coming and bothering me with the bullshit? The only people who like being out in those cages is these crazy-ass Mexicans,* thought Junebug. *Plus, I just want to lay down. I haven't had a good night's sleep in weeks. I keep waking up thru the night with Lisa on my mind. Ima sign up to see the mental doctor if this shit continue. Damn, I just wanna go home to Lisa and my daughter, but with all this time I got, that just don't seem possible. I keep telling everybody that I got action on my appeal, but truth be told, I became so frustrated with how Lisa was treating me, I forgot to file my shit in the required time limit—158 years with two life sentences.* Junebug thought as he lay down. "How the fuck they think a nigga can do all that?" he asked out loud to no one in particular. "How the fuck they think a nigga can do all that?" He asked once again and closed his eyes.

*** "Strip down and hand me your boxers," the c/o said. "Run your fingers along your gum line. Hold your hands out in front of you. Lift your nut sack. Okay, turn around. Let me see the bottom of your feet. Now squat like a catcher and give me two good coughs. Stand up and bend at the waist. Crack your ass cheeks. Okay, put your boxers and shower shoes on only," instructed the c/o.

*It's about time,* Cdog thought to himself. *They finally gon' get this search shit out the way.*
"Do you have anything in here illegal? Let me know now," said the c/o.
"Yeah, there's something illegal in my cell, muthafucka. Me," Cdog replied.
"Oh, we got a smartass, huh?" said another c/o. "I hope you remember how your photos look before they was sat in water," he said with a laugh.
"Man, do what you gon' do. This shit don't matter anymore anyway," replied Cdog while taking a memory picture of the c/o's face. *Yeah, this the one I want,* Cdog thought to himself. *Let's see if the picture in my mind of you is the same one the DA showed the jury.* Cdog looked at the c/o and smiled. "You got these cuffs tight as fuck on me," Cdog stated.

"That shit don't matter anymore, remember?" the c/o said and laughed. "Now get your ass to the benches and have a seat," he told him.

Cdog looked him square in the eye and winked, making the c/o turn his head. *Oh yeah, he the one,* Cdog thought. *He is the one.*

*** Later that day, Tank lay on his bunk in a semi-panic state of mind. *We will be off lockdown soon now that they searched our building. I need to put a plan together on how we gon' do this shit with the pigs. I can't let that nigga Cdog dictate how it goes down. I'm making my parole date, and I'm going to make Cdog pay for him disrespecting me.* "Yeah, nigga. I bet you don't see what's about to happen coming," Tank mumbled, thinking of Cdog. *The nigga sent me a kite after the search and said he got his target pick out already,* Tank thought. *Since that's the yard cop, I need to make sure it's only me, Cdog, and the c/o out there. I don't want nobody else to see how this shit go down.*

> *** Top of the day, my boy. Okay, we should be off lockdown soon. I feel you on that kite you sent me about having your target trip off this plan. Once we come off, all we gotta do is sign up to have our blood pressure checked. They will call us out together between eleven thirty and twelve thirty, which mean nobody will be out but us. The pig is the yard cop and always eats his lunch in the shade in between Blocks 2 and 3. That's also a blind spot from the yard tower.

Tank's kite went on to say how they should be able to get away.

*I'm not tripping off that,* Cdog thought as he tore the kite up and flushed it. *My concern is why all of a sudden, this nigga Tank want to do shit in the blind. He the nigga who always want to put a show on for muthafuckas, but fuck it. I'll go along with his plan and try to get away with it. Then I can focus back on my appeal to get my ass outta hell.*

> *** I've been back here for a couple months now,* thought Junebug. *I wonder what's up with Cdog and that bitch-ass nigga Tank. I guess they decided not to do shit after all. I know they still ain't on lockdown over there, right?* he asked himself. *I don't put this shit past Tank with his scary ass. He ain't nothing but talk, but I held Cdog higher than I do

*most niggas, even when my little brother said he was seeing Lisa in the car with Cdog. I never doubted that he was just giving her a ride somewhere because he is my homie, but now I don't know what to think of my boy,* Junebug thought as he sat down on the toilet. *If they send me back to this line, niggas gon' have to answer a few questions. He got back up and stood at the door.* "They look like they got a couple people on their way back here from the bed rolls they getting ready. Shit, it ain't nobody but some Mexicans," said Junebug out loud. "They the only ones coming to jail in jail," he said and bust out laughing. "Man, life in hell . . ." Junebug mumbled as he walked to his bunk.***

"So they say the blacks should be up starting tomorrow, but you know how they do shit," said Rosco through the vent to Cdog.

"Yeah, they say tomorrow but mean next week," Cdog replied with a chuckle.

"On the real," said Rosco. "Just wanted to let you know what I heard. You have a solid day."

"Good looking on that, and you do the same," Cdog said, and he stepped down from the vent.

A million things went through his mind at that moment. *I need to sign up to get my blood pressure checked. I need to get my thang off the yard. I need to make sure that nigga Tank is ready.* Thoughts were coming and going thru his mind so quickly, they made him lite headed. "I need a drink of water," he said out loud as he reached over to the locker for his cup.

It wasn't that Cdog was scared. It was that since he could remember, he always became panicked right before it was time to put work in. "Calm your ass down, Cdog," he said out loud. *It'll all be over soon.*

*** "On my momma, this shit about to go down," Tank said out loud. *We come up tomorrow, so they say, but in a couple days, this muthafucka will be back on slam status, for a year or longer this time,* thought Tank. *Fuck this yard anyway. The Mexicans been the only ones doing some active shit. Blacks wanna fistfight. These Mexicans playing with iron. That's one thing I gotta give to Cdog. He made sure he located and secured a few knives when he got here. I already had my shit, but the rest of these niggas is an entirely* *different story. What they gon' do once they don't have us around for security?* he asked himself.

"Turn your lights on and remove your window covers if you want to eat dinner," the c/o said over the building intercom.

"Yeah, let me get ready for the last meal," Tank said out loud, and he laughed.

*** "I wonder why this nigga keep sending me letters," Lisa asked her sister, Nesha. "I haven't wrote his dumb ass back in over five years."

"He sprung on your ass, that's why," replied Nesha.

"The nigga even had a nurse call here, talking about he might not make it."

This made them both burst out laughing for some reason.

"He didn't have them call his momma?" asked Lisa in between hitting the blunt.

"Hell naw, he didn't. Shit, his people didn't even know until I told them," said Nesha.

"But anyway, that nigga need to let me and my baby go," said Lisa.

"I'm only waiting on one nigga, and we both know who that is."

"Tank!" they screamed at the same time.

"You damn right," said Lisa. "In fact, I got two letters headed his way, and I need to JPay him some money. I be so glad when this is over and he come home."

"What's his release date?" asked Nesha.

"The nigga won't tell me. He just keep saying soon. I guess he's trying to sneak up on me," said Lisa. "Shit, I wish my real boo was coming home."

"Who? Junebug? I thought you just said fuck him," replied Nesha.

"Naw, bitch. I'm talking about little Cdog," said Lisa as she hit the blunt again.

"You really are a tramp, ain't you?" asked Nesha while laughing.

"You know it, little sis" answered Lisa. Then she added, "I got niggas ready to kill over this bomb pussy."

"Bitch, shut up and break down another blunt," said Nesha, which made them both laugh.

"But for real, that nigga Junebug need to leave us alone," stated Lisa. "Go wash your man's drawz or something. Ain't that what them ho-ass niggas do in there?"

"Girl, you know Junebug ain't no ho," replied Nesha. "Just write him and let him know to leave you alone."

> "Hell to the naw, bitch. So he can lie and tell Tank I'm writing him?" said Lisa. "Matter of fact, thinking about that nigga Junebug is fucking my high off. He made his bed, so why cry when it's time to lay in it? Fuck Junebug!" Lisa screamed. ***

"Fifteen minutes 'til yard. No Hispanics," said the building tower over the speaker.

*Finally, some fresh air*, thought Cdog. *I know all eyes will be on us for the first couple days, so maybe that nigga Tank right about doing shit the way he explain, but regardless, something must be done. I gotta keep my shit all the way gangsta at all times. I'm cut from an entirely different cloth than most niggas. Like Tupac said, "I won't deny it. I'm a straight rida. You don't wanna fuck with me."* Cdog rapped the lyrics while getting dressed for yard. *I hope that nigga Tank didn't tell anyone about our plans*, Cdog thought, standing at the door.

"Lights on if you coming out!" yelled the c/o on the tier.

"Top of the morning, fool," Cdog said to Tank as he walked up to him on the yard. "'Bout time they let a nigga out."

"Hell yeah," said Tank as the two embraced.

"Let's spin a few laps and catch up on what we got going," said Cdog.

"You don't want to wait on the rest of the homies to come out?" asked Tank.

"Shit, all my homies are already out here," Cdog said while looking Tank in the eye.

"I feel you, my boy, on that," Tank said with a smile.

As they walked around the track, they briefed each other on the situation they were both caught in.

"Lisa wrote me and said Junebug had sent her a few letters," said Tank. "The nigga even had someone call, talking about he might not make it and some other shit."

"I know the nigga think we forgot about him," stated Cdog. "Do you know if she holla back at him?"

"She didn't say, but I doubt she did. She been saying, 'Fuck that nigga.' She on your boy real tuff now. She ain't got time for him," said Tank with a smile, referring to himself.

"So she traded her baby daddy, who have life in prison, to be with his homie, who also have life in prison?" Cdog asked and knew from the look on Tank's face before he answered that it was about to be a lie.

"That nigga Junebug don't have the game I got," shot Tank. "But let's talk about something else, homie."

"Okay, I'm going to dig these thangs up tomorrow because the boy don't come back to work until the day after," said Cdog.

"That sound cool, but I still can't believe he got at you like that. He so fucking scary," replied Tank.

"Here come this nigga, Lil Man, so change the subject," said Cdog.

"They did kill that fool Smiley that day," said Tank.

"Yeah, I heard that too," Cdog said.

"Aye, what up with ya'll?" the fool Lil Man off the west side asked.

"Shit, not much," both Cdog and Tank mumbled at the same time.

"That's fucked up, what happen to Junebug," Lil Man said. "That's my goon right there."

"Shit, just another day in this life in hell, right?" Cdog asked.

That statement made Lil Man look up at Cdog because it was already a known fact around the yard that Cdog scared the shit out of him.

"Well, I just wanted to let ya'll know if you got anything on you, then put it up. The Woods supposed to deal with their own," Lil Man said.

"That's some bullshit," said Tank. "Them stupid muthafuckas had all the time. We were down to do that shit. Why put us back down when we just came out?"

"I don't know, Big Dog," Lil Man said to Tank, and then he added, "But shit, the police should know that have nothing to do with us."

"Aye, good looking out," Cdog told Lil Man.

Then he and Tank spun off.

"Now we gotta see how this play out," said Cdog.

"Yep. It may just be a two-on-one ass kicking with no weapons," replied Tank.

"You know damn well they try to keep up with the Mexicans, so yeah, they will be having weapons," said Cdog.

"Then let's make it back to our area," Tank said, looking around the yard for any sudden movement.

Almost as soon as they had made it to their table, the Woods made their move.

"Hey, help me!" screamed the white boy who was the target of the day. "Make them stop!" the white boy yelled as he tried to run away, only to be tackled by another Wood.

"They putting razors on his ass. Fuck a knife," said Tank. "He leaking like a muthafucka."

"Get down! Get down on the yard!" the gun tower yelled.

"Let's see if they shoot the Woods like they did the Mexicans," said Cdog.

"Hell naw, they ain't. You know better than that," said an OG named P-nut from the east side.

"Two on one, weapons involved!" one c/o barked into his walkie-talkie.

*Boom, boom, boom, boom, boom!*

"All they shooting is that bloc gun," said Tank. "Now they about to spray that Mace shit." Tank grabbed his T-shirt to cover his nose.

"They cutting his ass like a ham," P-nut said and made everybody in earshot laugh.

"Put your fucking hands behind your back now," said the c/o.

Both white dudes did.

"Inmates involved are in restraints. All weapons used have been recovered. We need medical to respond to the scene," the sergeant said in his walkie-talkie.

"Is that fool choking on his blood?" asked Tank.

"Shit, it look like it," replied P-nut.

"They rushing us off the yard like last time. They don't want any witnesses to them letting old boy die," said Cdog. "Tank, I'll catch you the next time they free us."

"Yep, fo' sho'," replied Tank.

*** *Oh yeah, I knew they had somebody coming back here*, thought Junebug. *I hope it's somebody I know.*

"Incoming!" one Mexican yelled down the tier.

June pressed his face against the door to look out the side toward the entrance of the building. "Man, them ain't nobody but some Woods," Junebug mumbled as he backed off the door. "Let me take my ass a nap." He lay down on the bunk. *I love sleep because I'm home with Lisa in my dreams.* "When I'm asleep and dreaming, it seem like I'm in heaven," he said to himself in a low voice. "But I return to life in hell when I wake up."

\*\*\* *See how that nigga tried to trap me on the yard when we was talking about Lisa?* Tank asked himself, *Why is the nigga so concerned with how much time I got and my appeal? I gotta watch that fool. He may be on some slick shit.* "But ain't no nigga slicker than me," Tank said out loud. *Plus, I'm starting to think the nigga ain't with what we got planned. If the c/o got at him how he said the fool did, then, nigga, you should've handled your business right then and there,* thought Tank. *Why wait for help? And I don't like how the nigga low key be punking my boy Lil Man.* "Man, just another day in this life in hell," Tank said in Cdog's voice. "Nigga, you ain't really with this life, so stop fronting." *But in the end, we gon' see how bad your ass is,* Tank thought and smiled.

\*\*\* Cdog was woken up from the sound of the building alarm. "What the fuck happen now?" he asked as he walked to his cell door.

"Open it up! Open it up!" a c/o was yelling, standing in front of a Mexican cell.

"Central control, be advised. Personal alarm in Building 4 is a medical. Please have medical respond," the sergeant said into his walkie-talkie.

*A fucking medical alarm, but look at these stupid muthafuckas in riot gear,* thought Cdog. *They got guns and shit like it's a full-fledged riot.*

"We need medical here now!" yelled a c/o. "Looks like a drug overdose."

"Yeah, that's what they known for," said Cdog to himself.

"No one goes in the cell until medical gets here," instructed the sergeant to the c/os.

Cdog stood at his door for what seemed to be an hour but was only ten minutes before he saw the medical staff come into the building.

"Right here," said the sergeant. "Possible drug overdose," he told medical as they went into the cell.

"Damn, they been in there for at least five minutes," said Cdog. "Why haven't they brought—"

Before he could finish the question of why they haven't brought the dude out, the medical staff had walked out of the cell, followed by the sergeant, who was talking into his walkie-talkie.

"Central control, be advised. Medical have pronounced the inmate DOA. Please route the ISU officers to the scene." He then looked up to the building tower and instructed, "Nobody in this entire building comes out of their cell for any reason until we get this sorted out."

*Wow*, thought Cdog. *Another one escapes the confinement of life in hell.*\***

*That nigga Junebug got the nerve to think I care about what happens to his ass in prison*, thought Lisa as she laid on her back, fucking her last trick of the night. *He left me and his daughter out here to fend for ourselves, so yeah, fuck Junebug and whateva he going through. Damn, I wish this nigga would hurry up and come. I got shit I need to do*, thought Lisa.

"Oh yeah, baby, right there," she moaned in the trick's ear, trying to help speed up the process of making him cum.

Twenty minutes later, Lisa found herself finally alone, so she pulled out her earnings for the evening and counted it. "Six hundred dollars," she said with pride in her voice. "I'm working the shit outta these lame-ass niggas." Then she smiled before going on to say "Gotta buy me, my daughter, and Nesha some shoes and then JPay my boo Tank a few dollars. I be glad when he come home. I won't have to turn tricks anymore." Lisa headed to the bathroom to take a shower. "I ain't gonna have to do this shit no more," she said to herself.

***

"Five minutes to yard," the tower cop said over the speaker. "No Hispanics."

"I knew they wasn't going to slam the whites," Tank said to himself. *That's cool though. I'm just glad they didn't keep us down. A white boy gets sliced the fuck up. Then a Mexican OD*, thought Tank. "It's really starting to feel like prison," he said, and he laughed. *I'm not going out to yard until after my phone call. I need to make sure Lisa put that money on my books.*

"Lights on if you coming out!" yelled a c/o.

"Aye, what it do?" Tank asked Cdog while standing in the dayroom.

"Shit, just chilling. I knew for sure we would be down a couple days," replied Cdog.

"Come on now. We both know how they treat the whites and others," Tank said, walking toward the phone.

"You ain't coming out?" asked Cdog.

"Yeah, but after my phone call," answered Tank.

"Okay, homie. Make sure you tell Lisa I said hello," Cdog said with a wink and smile.

"I'll let her know you said hello, but I don't know why the fuck you smiled and winked, my nigga," stated Tank.

"Turn that shit down, my boy. Just tell her I said hey," Cdog said as he turned to leave out of the building.

"Yeah, alrite, I'll tell her," said Tank, but he knew he wasn't going to tell her shit coming from Cdog.

He dialed Lisa's number, and after a couple of rings, the machine began to talk.

"You have a collect call from Tank. To accept, dial or say five now."

There was a two- or three-second pause before he heard, "To refuse this call, hang up, or to block inmate calls from this prison, press—" Tank hung up before the automated voice finished talking.

"Let me call this bitch one more time," Tank said to himself.

"You have a collect call from Tank. To accept, dial or say five now." This time, Tank heard, "Thank you for using Global Telink."

"Hey, baby. Y'all off lockdown?" asked Lisa.

"Yeah. Damn, why I gotta call twice before you accept?" Tank answered and asked a question.

"I didn't hear the phone ring the first time," lied Lisa.

*Who this bitch think I am? Junebug?* Tank said, "So how you doing?"

"I'm okay, just waiting on you, baby," she answered.

"Yeah, I can't wait to get there myself. Don't be out there giving my pussy away," said Tank.

"I'm not," Lisa said while thinking, *I'm not giving it away. I'm charging for this.*

"Were you able to JPay me that money for canteen?" asked Tank.

"Yes, baby. I did that a couple days ago," she answered.

"I haven't got the receipt yet, but good looking out," replied Tank.

"Baby, are you going to tell me when you get out?" Lisa asked.

"Soon," shot Tank. "You still got enough time to clean your shit up?" He laughed.

"There you go with that bullshit," she said.

"You have sixty seconds remaining," said the automated voice.

"I gotta go, but I'll call again soon," said Tank. "I love you, Lisa."

"Talk to you later," she replied. "I love you too."

Even the officer in the tower who was listening to their call smiled and said, "They both lying."

*** "Did you handle your business?" asked Cdog when Tank caught up with him on the yard.

"Yeah, I took care of it. I told her you said hello, and she said to tell you the same," Tank lied.

"Yep, fo' sho', but trip ain't nothing in the air right now, so this might be a good time to dig those thangs up," said Cdog.

"Okay. Handle that, and I'll keep security on you," replied Tank.

Cdog bent down to the spot he had buried the knives the day Smiley was killed. He moved the rock he had set on top of the hole he had put the knives in and began digging. After removing a couple of inches of dirt, Cdog felt what he was looking for. "They still here," he said to Tank. Cdog looked around the yard to be certain no one was watching before he continued digging up the weapons. "Ima take both of them in with me and tighten up the tips," said Cdog.

"Okay," said Tank. "Make sure mine is right."

"They always right, nigga," Cdog said with a laugh. "Don't forget to have the boy call us out day after tomorrow for the blood pressure check."

"Don't worry. I got my part down to a T," said Tank. "You just be ready between eleven thirty and twelve."

"I'm already ready," Cdog said with a smile on his face. "Ima slide my ass in before everybody else so I can put these up. I'll catch you later."

"Fo' sho'," replied Tank as they both walked off in opposite directions.

\*\*\* Cdog lay down on his bunk after sharpening the knives. He began to reflect on his past and wondered where the future would take him. *Man, I could've been anything I wanted*, thought Cdog. *Unlike most of the niggas I ran with, I had both my parents under the same roof who pushed me through school and made sure I always had what I needed. There wasn't a missing void in my life that most people say is the reason they joined a gang. I was popular with the females, cool with most niggas, and smart when it came to the books, but here I am, lying in this cell with a life sentence for a crime I didn't commit, but I'm not a snitch. I had to keep my mouth closed no matter how many times my momma said to tell the truth and come on back home. She couldn't comprehend the fact that coming back home wouldn't have been an option. If I told, we all would've became targets.* "Man, just let my appeal go through. I'm so done with the hood and even being around niggas from the hood," Cdog said loud enough only for him to hear. *Here's my problem. I have too much loyalty to shit that don't deserve it. Junebug, in reality, don't deserve what I'm about to do, but as a loyal soldier, I'll play my* *part in this shit.* "I be glad when this get over with," he mumbled before closing his eyes for a nap.

\*\*\* "Okay, homie. We set for tomorrow," Tank told Cdog as they walked around the track.

"Let's go over this shit one more time," said Cdog. "I want to do this right."

"We will be called out at eleven thirty." Tank started to unfold the plan. "Once we pass Block 3, we should see the boy sitting on the bench, eating lunch. Let me walk a few steps ahead of you so I can sneak up from behind and grab him so he can't push that button. Once you see I got him," Tank continued to explain, "you need to start booking his ass. We don't have much time before muthafuckas start walking by."

"So I will be the only one with a knife?" Cdog asked while feeling a panic attack about to take over his body.

"Yeah, nigga. I need to grab that fool so he can't run," replied Tank.

"After we finish, do we go to medical or back to the building?" asked Cdog.

"Shit, to be honest, I didn't think about that part," answered Tank. "But if you don't want to do it, then okay, we won't."

"Naw, naw, it's not like that. We doing this shit. I just need to know the plan," said Cdog.

"Shit, we can try to make it to medical," said Tank. "They never lock the front door during blood pressure check, but getting back to our cell is another story." Tank had no intentions of getting away, but he wanted Cdog to think he did. "So I'll see you around eleven thirty, I guess," said Tank, looking at Cdog.

"I'll be there, homie," replied Cdog.

"Fo' sho'," they both said as they pounded each other, fist to fist, and walked away.

Tank headed to the basketball court and Cdog to the law library.

\*\*\*

"Aye, youngsta, how you doing today?" asked Poppa, an OG off the east side who worked in the law library.

"I'm good, OG," replied Cdog. "I just need to know my next step on my appeal."

"Okay, tell me where you at," said Poppa.

Cdog ran down his situation and then showed Poppa the last letter he got from the courts saying they were granting the state their last and final request for an extension. "That's the last time I heard from them," said Cdog. "It's been about two months." "I don't want to get your hopes up or sell you a dream, youngsta, but the last time I seen this type of stuff happen, the dude ended up getting a letter from the courts like two or three months past the due date. He at home right now," said Poppa.

"Man, wouldn't that be nice?" replied Cdog.

"Hell yeah, it would," whispered Poppa, who rarely cussed. "Give it a little more time. Then come back if you haven't heard anything, and I'll help you get at them."

"I really appreciate that, OG," said Cdog as he looked Poppa in the face. "If you need anything out of canteen or a few dollars on your books, let me know."

"I'm good, youngsta, on all that," said Poppa as he leaned in a little closer. "Me helping you get out is my way of paying these folks back for the last thirty-four years they took from me." Poppa smiled. "Don't worry, I got you."

"All right, OG," said Cdog, and he laughed while turning to walk out the door.

*** Later that day, Cdog used the phone to call home.

"Hi, baby," said his mom once the call went through.

"Hi, Momma. It's sure good to hear your voice," said Cdog as his eyes became moist.

"Why do you wait so long to call us, Curtis?" his mother asked. "I be so worried about you."

"I'm alrite, Momma. I told you not to worry about me. I got this," replied Cdog.

"Boy, you ain't got nothing," his mom said in her scolding voice. "You got to give it to the Lord and let him have it."

"I know, Momma," Cdog said, now becoming irritated, which was the reason he barely called. "Have ya'll heard from the lawyer recently?"

"No, we haven't. Should we call him?" she asked.

He then went on to explain his situation about the letter from the courts and parts of the conversation he had had with Poppa.

"Well, like I said, Curtis, you gotta give it to the Lord," she stated. "No matter how bad you may want to come home or how bad we want you home, it won't happen until the Lord say it's time."

"I know, Momma" was all Cdog said.

"You got to pray, son. Don't be in there ashamed to bend your knees for the Lord. That's not how we raised you," his mother said.

"I only have one minute left on this call, so tell Dad I said hello. I love ya'll, and call the lawyer," Cdog said.

"We will, and we love you too," she replied in her motherly voice. "Remember to pray and give your situation to the Lord."

"I will do, Momma," he replied, but the call was already over.

As he hung the phone up, Cdog thought about how right his momma was when she said they were on the Lord's time. "That may be true, Momma," he said as he walked away from the phone, "but it's not the Lord keeping track of time in hell."

***

"Lights on if you want breakfast," the tower cop said over the speaker.

Cdog was already standing at his door, watching as they pushed the food carts in the building. He was looking for that disrespectful c/o. Then when he spotted him, Cdog smiled. "Yeah, your ass is mine," said Cdog to himself. The day had finally come for him and Tank to handle their business.

"If you eating, I need to see some lights," said a c/o.

"Naw, I'm good," replied Cdog.

His nerves were so bad at that moment, he wouldn't be able to eat if he wanted to. He was on his third cup of coffee and second shit of the day, but still, he wasn't hungry. He walked away from the door and started rapping the lyrics of his favorite rap group, the Ghetto Boys. "If it's going down, let's get this shit over with." Cdog laughed so hard and loudly that a c/o walking by with food trays stopped and looked into his cell.

"What's up?" Cdog asked.

The c/o answered a question with a question. "Just wondering—what's so funny?"

"You wouldn't get it if I told you," stated Cdog. Then he turned his back on the c/o, who was looking dumb as fuck.

\*\*\*

"If I open your door, then you need to report to medical," said the tower.

*Here we go*, thought Cdog as the door to his cell opened. Cdog double-checked where he had put the knife to be certain it couldn't be seen when he exited the building and to ensure he would have easy access to it once he reached his target. After being satisfied on how things looked, Cdog stepped out of the cell into the point of no return. He turned his head toward Tank's cell and saw that his door was open, but he had yet to step on the tier.

"Where this nigga at?" Cdog asked himself just as Tank stuck his head out the door.

"Give me a second," Tank said to Cdog.

"Ima be by the front door," replied Cdog. He was standing by the podium for about two minutes when Tank finally walked up.

"You ready?" he asked Cdog, looking nervous himself.

"Yeah, I'm as ready as I'll get," replied Cdog.

They both exited the building and began to walk toward Block 3. Just as Tank had planned, they were the only inmates on the yard. As they passed Block 3, they both spotted the c/o at the same time.

"Okay, let me get a few steps ahead of you," Tank said. "When you see me grab him, be ready to handle your business."

"I got you," said Cdog, starting to feel a panic attack creeping up on him.

Cdog fell about four steps behind Tank and watched as the c/o never even looked up as they approached. Cdog saw Tank make his move and grab the c/o around the neck just as he took a bite of his sandwich. He tried to pull Tank's arms away, but Tank was too strong for him. He couldn't yell for help because he still had the bite of sandwich in his mouth along with being choked by Tank. Cdog moved in just as the c/o remembered he had a panic button.

"Naw, muthafucka. You won't be pushing that," Cdog grabbed the c/o's hand. "Remember how my face look now?" Cdog said in a mocking voice.

As he began to push the knife into him, Cdog stabbed him in the face and head numerous times. Blood began to shoot out of every hole, right onto Cdog's clothes. Cdog watched as the c/o's eyes begin to roll as he lost consciousness. Tank, feeling the c/o's body go limp, let him go and then pushed him toward Cdog. Tank watched as Cdog tried to jump back but got his feet tangled with the c/o's, and they both fell to the ground, with the c/o on top.

"Get this fat fool off of me," said Cdog to Tank as he was now being drenched with the c/o's blood.

"Finish him off," said Tank as he looked around the empty yard.

Cdog was able to wiggle his arm from under the c/o and began to stab him in the side of his neck with the knife. "Okay, get his ass off me," Cdog told Tank for the second time.

Tank bent down and grabbed the c/o around the waist and tried to pull him up when his finger hit the c/o's panic button.

"Get down!" yelled the yard tower as he looked for the c/o whose alarm went off.

"What the fuck is going on?" yelled Cdog. "Get this fool off me!"

"They coming through the gate," said Tank as he was prone a couple of feet away from Cdog and the c/o. "Ain't nothing I can do." Tank said to Cdog as he watched the c/os run toward them.

"Don't you fucking move," a c/o told Tank as he ran by him to Cdog and the c/o on the ground. "Officer down! Officer down!" the c/o yelled into his walkie-talkie. "Staff assault with weapon." He looked down at his fellow officer and saw all the blood coming from multiple holes. "Don't resist!" yelled the c/o as he began to stomp the arm and hand of Cdog that still held the knife.

"Let the knife go," ordered the sergeant to Cdog.

*Damn*, Cdog thought to himself. *Caught red-handed.* "Here, man!" Cdog yelled as pain shot up his arm.

The sergeant kicked the knife out of arm's reach and then told Cdog to keep his hand where it can be seen. They couldn't beat Cdog's ass like they all wanted to because the officer was still on top of him.

"Secure him in cuffs!" barked the sergeant while pointing at Tank.

"I didn't do nothing," said Tank.

"Shut the fuck up," said a c/o as he put all his weight on Tank's back with his knee.

"We need medical," said the sergeant into his walkie-talkie. "We need them now! Officer down!" he screamed.

Numerous c/os now stood around the scene, waiting for the opportunity to get their blows in on Cdog.

"Take that one to the cage in program," said the sergeant, pointing at Tank.

A c/o bent down and grabbed the chain of the cuffs that were on Tank and pulled up. Tank screamed out in pain as the already-too-tight cuffs began to cut his wrists.

"Stop resisting," said a c/o as he kicked Tank in his side, knocking the wind out of him. "Get your ass up!" yelled the officer who was still pulling on the cuffs as they carried and half-dragged Tank toward the program office.

"Okay, let's roll the officer off him," instructed the sergeant to the c/os after an ISU officer had finished taking photos.

"Keep your hands right where they are," said the c/o who was standing on Cdog's right hand.

Cdog watched as they rolled the officer off him. His body tensed up, ready for the blows he knew were coming.

"Roll on your stomach!" yelled the sergeant.

Cdog hesitated for a second because he knew once he was facedown, he wouldn't be able to protect himself from their beating.

"Roll your ass over," said a c/o as he kicked Cdog in the side of his face.

"Hold it," said a female voice. "We doing this one by the book."

Cdog looked up at the lady who had gold bars hanging from her shirt collar.

"Keep this scene secure just as it is," she ordered. "Sergeant, I want you to start taking photos of everything in this area. If you see an ant with blood on it, I want to see it on a picture."

Cdog, now cuffed and sitting up, realized that medical wasn't working on the officer who was still lying on the ground. Cdog began to look around at the c/os, and they all had the same looks on their faces: the look of pain from a serious loss. *Damn. Is this fool dead?* Cdog asked himself.

"You lucky the lieutenant is here," said a c/o, looking at Cdog with hate and disgust. "She won't be around all the time." The c/o walked away.

"After you are done with the photos, escort this inmate to medical and then to my office," the lieutenant said to the sergeant.

Cdog watched as the officers put the knife inside an evidence bag and thought to himself how he wished he could've gotten rid of that. *Plus, that nigga Tank wasn't any kind of help. He lay down almost right after the alarm went off. Who pushed the button anyway?* Cdog asked himself.

"Stand up," said a c/o as he grabbed Cdog by the arm.

"Look this way," instructed the sergeant to Cdog.

Another c/o held the bag with the knife in it up to Cdog's chin as the sergeant began to snap photos.

"Okay, escort him to medical," said the sergeant to a c/o. "After he is done there, put him in the cage in the program office."

"Let's go," said the c/o's eyes as he snatched Cdog by the cuffs.

Cdog held his head high as he was being led away. He met each c/o's eyes as he walked past them and saw the hate that was inside of them. Cdog knew at that point that had it not been for the lieutenant, he wouldn't be walking off the yard but carried. He looked down just as he was passing the c/o on the ground and realized what he had just done. "Damn" was all he could mumble to himself.

*** "It says here that you have a parole date coming up soon," said the lieutenant to Tank, who was being interviewed after leaving medical, "so why would you just throw that away?"

"I didn't do nothing," Tank replied. "I was on my way to get my blood pressure checked when the yard went down."

"Look, Adams, we gonna cut out all the bullshit because we both know that you were involved in what went down with my officer. Your file tells me that you and Johnson are from the same gang, so don't try to feed me crap and tell me it's steak," said the lieutenant.

"I didn't do nothing," Tank said again.

"Okay, if you want to spend the rest of your life in prison, then stick to that story," the lieutenant replied, "but if you want to see another day in the free world, then you gotta help me help you."

"If I knew something, I would tell you," Tank said, "but I don't."

"When you lying your ass in that cell and the walls feel like they closing in on you, that's when I want you to remember that I tried to help you," she said.

The image of him lying in the cell suddenly flashed in his mind, and it gave him chills. He knew that the lieutenant didn't lie when she said he would spend the rest of his life in prison for what had happened with the c/o. *That nigga Junebug or Cdog ain't worth that*, thought Tank, *but I'm not a snitch.*

"I don't have anything else to say," Tank told the lieutenant. "I didn't do anything."

"If that's how you want to play this, I have no problem with that," she told him, "but if you change your mind . . ." She winked and smiled. "Take him to the cage and bring Johnson in," she told a c/o.

*** Cdog watched as the c/o put Tank in the holding cell and knew his turn to be interviewed would be next. "I know my boy didn't tell them shit," Cdog said to himself, but a bad feeling shot through his body at the same time.

"Turn around and stick your hands out the slot," a c/o told Cdog, snapping him from the thought he was having about Tank.

He turned and put his hands out to be cuffed when he felt a hand grab each of his wrists. He tried to pull his hands back but couldn't.

"What the fuck ya'll doing?" he yelled, asking the c/os.

"Shut up, you piece of shit," one of the c/os said. "You will not have another comfortable day as long as you are in this prison," one of the c/os told Cdog in a whisper just as another c/o snapped his index finger back, breaking it instantly.

Cdog screamed out in pain, but that didn't stop the c/os from breaking another finger.

"Stop trying to fight us!" yelled the sergeant over Cdog's screams.

"I'm not fighting ya'll!" screamed Cdog. "My fucking fingers are broken!" Cdog felt the cuffs being placed on his wrists so tightly, they cut off the circulation of blood to his hands.

"When this cage door opens up, don't do shit except back your ass out," said the sergeant. "Do you understand my order?"

"Yeah, man, I hear you," Cdog replied in pain.

"Open the cage," the sergeant told one of the c/os.

Cdog began to move backward slowly when the cage door opened.

"Keep coming back," said one of the c/os.

Cdog turned his head to the left toward the c/o's voice when he felt numerous hands grab him and slam him face-first to the ground.

"I told you not to do nothing but back your ass out the cage," said the sergeant.

Cdog opened his mouth to say he just wanted to ask to see the nurse, but he couldn't move his jaw. Cdog felt the hands and feet of the c/os holding him down, so he couldn't move. Unable to do anything else, Cdog laid his head on the floor and let the blood run from his mouth.

"We need medical to respond to the program office," said the sergeant into his walkie-talkie.

A few moments later, the lieutenant walked in and asked, "What happened?"

"When we opened the cage door, he tried to attack us," lied the sergeant, "so we took him down."

Cdog, unable to say a word, listened to the lie being told to the lieutenant.

"I told you I wanted this to be by the book," said the lieutenant to the sergeant. "Now you adding bullshit to complicate this situation. He got his fucking hands cuffed, but you say he tried to attack you and about, what, seven more officers?' she asked, looking around the room.

"He tried to attack us," said the sergeant in a matter-of-fact kind of voice.

"Don't tell me that crap again!" yell the lieutenant. "I want your report of the entire incident up to now ASAP, and you can brief the yard sergeant on the situation because I'm relieving you of your duties as of right now. You can also guarantee this will be investigated by an outside source, and if you are found to be at fault, I will personally do all in my power to have you prosecuted for assault."

"You do what you feel needs to be done lieutenant," said the sergeant, "but you keep in mind that we just carried one of our own off the yard because of this piece of shit." He was pointing down at Cdog.

"I'm aware of what he did, and he will pay for it, but I didn't want it to go this way. Now contact the yard sergeant so we can wrap this up," the lieutenant said as she walked away.

The sergeant bent down to Cdog's ears and whispered in a low voice, "Don't think this is over, boy. I'm just getting started."

"Medical is here," said a c/o to the sergeant.

Cdog looked up at the sergeant and wanted to spit in his face or scream at him, but he couldn't open his mouth. *Damn*, thought Cdog. *My jaw is broken, and I lost a tooth. You right, Sergeant, you bitch-ass muthafucka. This ain't over.*

"Can you tell me what happened?" asked the medical staff to Cdog. "Where do you hurt at?"

All Cdog could do was let out a muffled sound to the nurse, which made the sergeant and a few c/os laugh.

"Once I'm done with the incident report, I'll walk over a copy," said the sergeant to the nurse, "but to make it short and simple, he tried to attack us when we opened up the cage, so we took him to the ground."

"I have to call for transport," said the nurse. "I think his jaw could be broken." The nurse made a quick call on the office phone and then came back into the room where the cages were. She went right to Cdog. "Can you open your mouth at all?

Cdog shook his head, and pain shot through his whole body from the simple head movement.

The nurse saw the look on his face and told him not to move again or try to talk. "I gotta go make another call," said the nurse to the sergeant. "Try to not move him."

Once the nurse went out of the room, the sergeant bent down again to Cdog's ear and whispered, "This ain't nothing compared to what I have planned for you, nigger. I own you now, boy, and you will pay for what you done to my friend."

Cdog, unable to say a word, just closed his eyes and hoped that the blows wouldn't start coming. He felt relief when he heard the lieutenant's voice.

"They are going to take him to outside medical for treatment. I need you to start your report," the lieutenant said to the sergeant.

"Yes, Madam Lieutenant," said the sergeant sarcastically as he stormed out.

"As of right now, we are on full lockdown. There's no inmate movement, period," she said to the c/os. "Get this blood off the floor and have the paperwork done to admit Inmate Robinson—I mean, Adams—to Ad Seg." She began to walk out the room but stopped when her eyes made contact with Tank. "Before you do anything with Inmate Adams, have him brought back to my office first." She walked off.

***

Cdog, now in the institution van on his way to the hospital, had never felt so much pain before. *It fucking hurts to breathe, and it hurts to swallow my spit*, thought Cdog. *Man, I hope to get the chance to put hands on that bitch-ass sergeant. He the one who slammed me to the ground. That lieutenant bitch think she half as slick. All she really concerned with is making sure our ass get booked, so I hope Tank didn't fall for her bullshit and told her something they could use against us. He kinda stupid like that when it come to a bitch.* Cdog leaned his head back and closed his eyes in prayer. He prayed that God would stop the pain he was feeling in his face and head and to be forgiven for the murder he had just committed. *Damn*, Cdog thought as he opened his eyes. *What the fuck have I done?*

*** "I don't know why ya'll keep bringing me in here!" screamed Tank. "I told you I had nothing to do with that out there."

"I'm not going to ask you about what happened on the yard earlier. I'll let the detectives question you about that," said the lieutenant.

"Detectives? Why would I have to talk with them when I didn't do anything?" asked Tank in a nervous voice.

"Because all you keep telling me is you haven't done anything, and we both know that's a lie, but let me say again that's not why I had them bring you back in here," she said. "I want to know if you saw what happened to Inmate Johnson when the officers opened the holding cage."

"Is he all right?" asked Tank.

"Broken fingers, a lost tooth, and his jaw may be broken, but he will live," said the lieutenant. "If my officers were wrong, I need to know."

Tank looked up at the lieutenant and then at the two c/os who were on each side of him. Then he looked back at the lieutenant but didn't say a word.

"You don't have to be afraid to tell me the truth," said the lieutenant. "These are some of my trusted officers, so nothing will happen to you for this, I guarantee it."

Tank looked around the room one more time before he spoke. "Yeah, I seen that shit," said Tank, "and it wasn't right."

"Tell me what you saw," said the lieutenant.

"And what do I get if I do?" asked Tank.

"How about the chance to help your homie out?" she said "I can't promise you anything other than that."

Tank realized what he saw happen wasn't going to change his situation at all, but it would fuck that sergeant who did the shit over. "It was that sergeant," said Tank. "I watched him open that cage after they broke Johnson's fingers and had Johnson to back out, but as he was about to step out, that sergeant grabbed him by his neck and slammed him to the ground face-first."

"Did you see anything else?" asked the lieutenant. "How about the other officers?"

"Naw, the sergeant was the only one I saw do something," lied Tank.

"At any time, did you see Johnson rushing towards the officers?" the lieutenant asked.

"No" was all Tank said.

"I thank you for being honest with me," said the lieutenant, "but you will be going to Ad Seg for the incident earlier. They will sort everything out for you back there."

"What am I being charged with?" asked Tank.

"Nothing right now. We have to do our investigation, but until then, I have no choice but to remove you from the general population," the lieutenant said.

"How long will the investigation take?" asked Tank.

"I would only be guessing if I told you an answer to that question," she said. "Okay, put him back in the holding cage until the paperwork is done."

***

"Open cell 136!" yelled the floor cop to the control booth.

Junebug walked to his cell door and watched as the c/o put a bedroll and a mattress inside cell 136. "Got somebody coming in," Junebug said out loud to himself. *I bet it's just another one of these Mexicans. They seem to be the only muthafuckas coming back here*, thought Junebug, who turned from the door and walked to his bunk, where he sat down and once again thought about what had brought him back there. "Those niggas Tank and Cdog," he said out loud. "Them fools was popping their lips talking like they were ready to get active, but here I sit, by myself."

Then his mind went to Lisa, which made him lie down on his bunk and close his eyes. Lately, he had been fighting to keep thoughts of her out of his head because they made him feel like a depressed case. "I gotta be strong," he whispered as he lay on the bed, trying to fight his thoughts, but as always, thoughts of Lisa won. "I love you so much, Lisa," he said out loud. "I don't know why you treat me like this."

He continued to lay on his bunk as his mind begin to flash memories of Lisa like a video in his head. A smile formed on his lips as a picture of him and her at the pier flashed thru. "Man, I can remember that day like it just happened yesterday." The memory began to take over. "Let's go get on the roller coaster," he said out loud in the cell, now completely caught up in his thoughts, talking to Lisa like they were still on the pier. "Ima win you a teddy bear when we get off the ride," he said as he brung his knees to his chest, making his body look like a big ball on the bunk. "Ima win you a teddy bear," he said once again as tears began to roll down his face.

"I will always love you, Junebug" was the last thing he'd heard in his mind as he forced himself to sleep.

*** Cdog lay in the hospital bed, looking up at the ceiling. *Fuck*, he thought to himself, *my jaw and finger are broke. Plus, I'm now missing a tooth. That bitch-ass sergeant better hope I never come face-to-face with him again 'cause* *his ass is mine.* Cdog tried to smile from the thought of beating up the sergeant's ass, but the pain in his jaw wouldn't allow him to. *Somebody gon' pay for this shit,* Cdog thought to himself. *Don't they know every dog has its day? And by me, being Cdog, I got two days. I already used one on that bitch-ass c/o. Ima save the other one for you, Sergeant.*

Cdog looked toward the door to see if he saw a nurse. He needed another one of those shots that put him out earlier. All Cdog saw were two c/os sitting by the door, reading the newspaper. Cdog made a loud groaning sound to get their attention. They both glanced his way but went back to their newspaper. Cdog groaned again but this time louder. One of the c/os finally got up and walked toward him.

"What the fuck you want?" asked the c/o in a whisper.

Cdog, unable to talk, pointed to his jaw with his hand not cuffed.

"Oh, now I get it. Your ass need something for the pain," said the c/o as he looked at the door. He turned his eyes back to Cdog, and all Cdog saw was hate in them. "What I'm about to give you can be given as often as you need it." The c/o smiled.

Then he slapped Cdog so hard on his jaw, it brought tears to his eyes, and blood ran out his nose. Cdog, unable to say a word, groaned out of pain.

"Let me know when you need another one," said the c/o as he walked back to his seat.

Cdog used his free hand to cover his nose to stop the bleeding. He couldn't, however, stop the tears from coming out of his eyes, mixed with pain and anger. His jaw begin to throb from the slap, and that made him cry more. *This muthafucka straight just slapped me like I was a bitch,* thought Cdog as his eyes went back to looking at the ceiling. *I won't be like this forever,* he thought. *I won't be like this forever . . .*

*** "Stop fighting and get down on the floor!" yelled the c/o, which woke Junebug out of his trance. "Get your ass off him now!" the c/o continued to yell.

Junebug hopped off his bunk and walked to his cell door. He looked through the side crack and saw where all the commotion was coming from. The dudes three cells down from him were fighting. The c/o opened the tray slot on the cell door and began to spray his can of Mace inside the cell. Another c/o followed suit while yelling for the inmates to stop fighting.

Junebug grabbed his towel and soaked it in water before wrapping it around his mouth and nose.

"Stop fighting and get down!" the c/os yelled for the third time, and for the third time, a can of Mace was emptied in the cell.

"Both of ya'll stay on the ground," ordered the Ad Seg sergeant. "Be ready to open the door," he told the tower officer.

"You right here, stand up and back up to the fuckin' door," a c/o ordered one of the dudes.

Junebug watched as about nine c/os stood outside the cell, waiting for the door to open.

"Lock your hands behind your neck," the sergeant said. "Okay, it's clear to open!" he yelled to the tower.

Junebug continued to watch, even though the Mace was now kicking his ass. The door to the cell opened and closed just as fast, and Junebug saw one of the dudes being slammed to the floor.

"Put your hands behind your back!" yelled the c/os.

"I can't," said the dude. "Y'all standing on my arms."

After a few seconds on the ground and now with the cuffs on the dude, the c/os snatched the dude off the floor and led him to one of the cages.

"Back up to the tray slot and stick your hands out," said the sergeant to the other inmate. "Open the door!" he yelled after the cuffs were on the second inmate. "Take him straight to medical."

Junebug looked at the dude as they walked past his cell. *Look like that nose is broken*, Junebug said to himself. "Oh, well. I guess the show is over," he said out loud as he went to sit on his bunk. "Woke me up with this bullshit!" he yelled toward the door as he lay back down with the towel still on his face.

***

"Let's go, Adams. Your ride's here," said the c/o. "Turn around and stick your hands thru the slot."

Tank did as instructed and felt the cold steel handcuffs being placed around his wrists.

"This is your copy of the lockup order," one of the c/os said as he put the papers into Tank's hands.

"What about the other dude?" asked Tank, referring to Cdog. "Is he already back there?"

"No," answered one of the c/os. "He will be on a later ride."

This made all the c/os laugh.

Tank, who didn't get the inside joke, just stared at the c/o whom the lieutenant, about ten minutes ago, said was one of her trusted officers. *I knew I should not have told that bitch nothing about the sergeant*, thought Tank. *These muthafuckas might beat my ass now.*

"Central control, be advised. We got one 10-15 from Delta Yard en route to Ad Seg," said a c/o into his walkie-talkie.

"Ten four. Central control copy," came the response.

They put Tank inside a van and drove for maybe forty-five seconds, but to Tank, it felt more like two hours. *Damn, this ride feels similar to how I felt when they drove me to the substation*, Tank thought. "But I'll be damned if this ride have the same outcome," Tank mumbled, referring to all the time he had received from that ride to the substation.

"What you say?" asked the c/o who heard him mumble.

"I said that this is a long-ass ride to be going nowhere," Tank replied, playing it off.

"Why do they all say that?" asked the c/o to another c/o, who just hunched his shoulders.

"Maybe it's because all ya'll do is drive us in a circle inside this square-like box ya'll got us living in," said Tank, referring to the design of the prison.

"Well, we're sorry we disappointed you with how your forty-acre compound turned out," said the pale-faced c/o with a loud laugh, "but don't worry. You will be in your warm bed soon enough."

Then all three c/os laughed.

"Fuck all ya'll," said Tank, "especially you, Powder Face," he said to the pale face one.

"We will see how your attitude changes in a month after being in Ad Seg," said Pale Face.

"I'm not tripping," said Tank. "All this shit is the same."

They pulled up to the back of the Ad Seg building, and the c/o opened the van door and then ordered Tank to get out. Tank stepped out and was greeted with the sight of what appeared to be dog cages at a kennel. The Ad Seg c/o told Tank to step inside one. Once the door to the cage was closed and locked, he told Tank to stick his hands through the slot so the handcuffs could be removed. Tank watched as the c/os who had brought him there drove off.

The Ad Seg officers then began their ritual of having him strip naked so a body search could be performed, which ended with a c/o ordering Tank to squat and give them three good coughs. Tank was then told to get dressed in socks, boxers, a T-shirt, and shower shoes.

"The last thing we need to say," said one of the c/os, "is this. We don't know how long you will be back here or how long it will take to receive your write-up. That's all up to the staff on the yard you came from, so don't ask us about any of that shit." The c/o stopped talking so what he had just said could sink into Tank's brain. Then he continued with his speech. "Back here, for the first ten to fourteen days, you don't have nothing coming but a shower every forty-eight hours. Once you are classified, you will be clear to attend yard." He waved around to let Tank know this was the yard. "Property also only comes once you are classified. If you got a homie back here, the answer is always no on passing shit for ya'll. We don't do it, so don't ask," said the c/o, now sounding like he had given that speech a million times.

"Do you have any questions?" asked another c/o.

"No, I don't," replied Tank. "He answered them already."

"So since you understand what he just told you, let's get you to your cell," said the c/o. "We will make sure it's ready, so just hang here for a few."

Tank watched as they went into the building. *What the fuck have I gotten myself in?* Tank asked himself as he took a look around at all the cages. "This some shit for animals," he said. "Yeah, I can't see myself back here too long." Then he sat down on the sink that was in the cage and waited for them to come get him. *Damn*, thought Tank once again and began to look around at what they called the yard. "I was already living my life in hell," mumbled Tank, "but this shit right here is the belly of hell."

\*\*\*

"The shots that killed Mr. Smith came from the passenger side of the car, as testified by numerous witnesses," said the DA to the jury. "Based on the evidence, you have no other choice except to find Mr. Johnson guilty."

"After being found guilty by a jury of your peers, I hereby sentence you to life in prison without the possibility of parole," said the judge.

Cdog opened his eyes and realized that once again, he was having the same nightmare that had woken him up many times since walking out of the courtroom. He now knew that he was in the hospital when his jaw began to hurt like hell. He grabbed his jaw with his free hand and remembered being slapped like a bitch by the c/o. Cdog raised his head off the pillow to look toward the door. He saw the two c/os. Cdog rattled the bed bar with his cuff hand to get the c/os' attention. They both looked his way with suspicion before one of them got up and walked to the bed. Cdog used his free hand to point to the restroom.

"Oh, you need to use the toilet?" the c/o said but made it sound like a question.

Cdog gave him a thumbs-up.

The c/o turned to his partner and, in a mocking child voice, said, "Little man gotta go potty." Then he laughed.

The other c/o stood up and looked down the hall to motion for the hospital cop, who was the only one allowed to be armed on the floor. Once the officer reached the door, the c/o began to uncuff Cdog's hand.

"Straight to the toilet and back," said the c/o, stepping aside to allow Cdog to get out of the bed.

"Don't try no funny shit, or you will be taken down," a c/o said as Cdog walked past him.

Cdog, unable to talk, just shook his head but thought, *I'm about to break this fool's shit for that slap earlier.* Cdog spun and hit the c/o so fast and hard that the other c/o and hospital cop hesitated long enough for Cdog to get one more punch in, which broke the c/o's nose and put him to sleep at the same time. Cdog watched as the c/o hit the floor, with blood gushing out of his nose.

"Get your ass on your knees!" ordered the hospital cop, who now had his weapon out and pointed at Cdog. "I don't know what ya'll got going on at that prison, but right now, you at my place of business. Don't make me shoot you. Get on your knees now!" the hospital cop yelled.

Cdog bent to his knees and went to raise his hands in the air when he felt the first blow from the other c/o's baton. Before Cdog could react to the first blow, another one came but this time to the side of his face. Cdog was knocked out instantly and didn't feel the next five to six blows that followed. Nor did he hear the conversation between the c/o and the hospital cop.

"Why didn't you shoot him?" asked the c/o. "We already told you we have the go to shoot to kill him if he tries anything."

"Yeah, I know, but it happened so fast, I couldn't get a clear shot," replied the hospital cop.

"The chance to kill this piece of shit will happen again. I just hope I'm there when the time comes," the c/o said with hate and disgust in his voice.

\*\*\* "Incoming!" yelled the inmates who were standing at their doors.

This was a tradition played out every time a new inmate was brought into Ad Seg. Hearing that call would bring almost everyone to their door to see if it was someone they knew. Junebug, lying on his bunk, caught up in a daze over Lisa, didn't really hear the call, so he didn't see Tank come in, but one of the Mexicans back there for killing Smiley saw him. *Bang, bang* came the sound from Junebug's ceiling. Junebug got up and stepped to his cell vent because he already knew who was banging.

"Aye, what it do, Cyclone?" asked Junebug through the vent.

"Excuse me for bothering you, ay, but I think they just came in with one of your people," the Mexican replied.

*Why the fuck is this fool banging on the wall like I care if they brought a nigga back here?* thought Junebug, but he said "Oh yeah?" instead.

"The only reason I'm telling you is because it look like it could've been your homie Tank," said Cyclone.

"*Tank?*" Junebug said in a question-and-statement kind of tone.

"By the time I got to the door, I barely saw him, but I know that fool walk, ay," said the Mexican. "They put him somewhere in that back corner toward C-section."

"Tank?" Junebug repeated in the same tone he had used the first time.

"But anyway, I just wanted to let you know. You have a good day down there," said Cyclone.

"Good looking out," said Junebug, still sounding confused. "You have a good day likewise up there."

"Thank you," said Cyclone.

"Yep," replied Junebug as he stepped down from the vent. He walked to his cell door and looked around, but there was no movement. "Shit, the only way I'll know if it was him for sure is in two days, when the captain comes for interviews," Junebug mumbled to himself. He looked through the side of his door that faced the yard. "How the fuck did I miss that?" Junebug asked himself out loud, but he already knew the answer.

*Lisa . . . Man, I gotta snap outta this trance she got me in*, thought Junebug. *I'm missing shit I know I supposed to see, but I love her so much, I can't think of nothing else but her most of the time.* Junebug turned from his cell door and walked to his bunk. He lay down on the bottom bed and looked up to the top bed, where he had hung the only picture he had of Lisa. "I love you so much," Junebug said to the photo in a low voice. "We will be a family again." He closed his eyes, not even aware that tears were running down his cheeks.

He rolled onto his side and balled his body up, allowing his mind to once again take him back to a moment he shared with Lisa.

"You don't have to worry, baby. I will always have your back," Junebug heard her say in his mind.

"Shit, these muthafuckas about to give my black ass triple life plus fifty-seven years," he told her.

"That don't matter. Ima be by your side, walking that shit off with you until your appeal go through," she told Junebug.

"That's why I love your ass," Junebug said into the jail telephone. "I knew you were the one for me."

"I got you, my nigga," Lisa said.

Junebug, who was still in a ball on his bunk, smiled as his mind replayed that conversation. "I love you," he mumbled to the walls of his cell. He rolled over on his back and looked up at Lisa's photo. "I love you," he said once again then closed his eyes for sleep.

***

Six hours after the assault, Cdog woke up to nothing but pain and darkness. He tried to raise his hand to touch his head because that was where the most pain was coming from. His hand stopped in midair with a rattle, so he tried the other one but had the same result. Both his feet were also chained to the hospital bed.

"By orders of the warden, you will remain cuffed at all times while here in the hospital," said a voice.

Cdog turned his head from side to side but couldn't see anything because of the darkness.

"The staff here at the hospital had to wrap your head and face due to the fall you took after assaulting another officer," said the voice.

*A fall?* Cdog asked himself. *That muthafucka whipped my ass.*

"There is a pan under your ass, so feel free to piss or shit when you want to," the voice told Cdog. "Now due to the fall, your jaw is not only broken but shattered in more than six places, which requires major surgery to repair. I'll be at the door, so rattle your cuff if you need anything."

Cdog heard the footsteps as they left his bed. *Okay,* he thought, *I got a few days here.* He would've smiled if he was able to as he dropped a turd into the pan.

Three days later and after his surgery, Cdog was ready to once again return to the hell he had come from to face the music from his actions. *I will be going straight to the hole,* thought Cdog, *but even that will be better than being chained to a bed all fucking day. Plus, I can sit my ass on a toilet to take a shit.* The last thought made him smile a little, which didn't hurt as much than before the surgery. *Yeah, I'm on my way back.* Cdog closed his eyes for a nap.

***

Tank stood in the middle of his cell and looked around—a bunk, a toilet, a sink, and a desk. "This some depressing shit right here," Tank whispered as he moved toward the bunk and bedroll. Halfway into making up his bunk came three or four loud bangs on the wall. Tank knocked back twice and then asked, "What's the deal?"

"Aye, I'm Sniper, and my cellie is Joker," came the reply.

*So they got me next to some Mexicans,* Tank thought. "Okay, fo' sho'. They call me Tank," he said.

"Are you active?" asked the Mexican.

"Yep, I just came from D-yard," answered Tank.

"Cool then, homie. We came off C-yard about eight months ago for an assault," said the Mexican.

*I'm not about to discuss shit with these fools on why I'm in here,* thought Tank, so he changed the subject. "Is any of my people close by?" he asked.

"Where you from?" asked the Mexican.

"I'm black, homie. Is there any other black in this area?" snapped Tank.

"Aye, I didn't mean any disrespect when I asked where you were from," said the Mexican. "But yeah, there's two blacks on this side, but they came off A-yard."

Tank immediately knew they were SNY if they came from A- or B-yard because those were the prison's two sensitive-needs yards (SNY). "Do you know where or if there's a black dude back here named Junebug?" asked Tank.

"Naw, I haven't heard no one call that name out over the tier since I've been back here," the Mexican answered.

"Okay, that's what's up. I'm about to finish making my bunk," Tank said.

"You have a good night, and if you need anything, just knock on the wall," said the Mexican.

"Likewise," said Tank, exchanging one bogus invitation with theirs. Tank walked to his bunk to finish making it up. Once done, he lay down, and before he knew it, he was out cold.

Two hours later, Tank was jolted from his sleep.

"Lights on if you want to eat!" yelled the c/o once again.

"I'm good!" screamed Tank from his bunk. Tank watched as the c/o put the tray back on the cart and pushed it toward the next cell.

"I got a refusal from cell 246!" yelled the c/o to the gun tower cop, who, in return, wrote it down in the logbook.

After the cart went a few cells down, Tank heard a knock on the wall. *What the fuck this Mexican want now?* thought Tank as he got up off the bed and walked toward the door. Once there, Tank knocked back on the wall.

"Aye, sorry to bother you," said the Mexican, "but I noticed you didn't take your dinner."

"Yeah, I'm cool on that shit," said Tank.

"Well, just so you know, back here, after three times you don't eat, the c/ os send medical to talk to you," he said. "If you refuse your food or sleep too much, they think you doing through depression."

"Naw, it ain't no shit like that with me at all," said Tank. "I just didn't want to get my ass up."

"I feel you, but I just wanted to let you know how they get down. You have a good evening over there," said the Mexican.

"Thank you, and ya'll have a good night also," Tank replied and walked back to his bunk. *I can't see myself being back here for too long,* thought Tank as he looked around the empty cell. "I'm in jail, in jail," Tank whispered to himself with a slight sarcastic smile.

Tank got off his bunk and walked back to the door, where he looked out toward the few cells he could see. "Where is that nigga Junebug?" Tank mumbled to himself. "I know his dumb ass still back here." Tank ran his eyes over the part of the building he could see, but he was too far to read the nametags on any of the cell doors.

"Now that I think about it, this shit is depressing," Tank said as he walked back to his bunk and lay down. "The captain need to come holla at me," he mumbled.

***

*It is that fool,* thought Junebug two days later, standing at his cell door and watching Tank walk into the office for his seventy-two-hour lockup hearing with the captain. "I wonder what that nigga did," Junebug asked himself in a low voice.

*Boom, boom* came the sound from Junebug's ceiling.

He stepped up to his vent and yelled, "Aye, top of the day to you, fool!"

"Same to you, my boy," said Cyclone. "They got your homie Tank in the office."

"Yeah, I see him," replied Junebug.

"Alrite then. I just wanted to let you know that," said Cyclone. "You have a good day down there. I'm gone"

"Likewise to you, fool," said Junebug as he stepped down from his vent and went back to the door.

After about thirty minutes of standing at his door, Junebug start having a bad feeling as to why it was taking Tank so long to come out of that office. "That nigga sure seem to be doing a lot of explaining," Junebug mumbled to himself. "What the fuck have you gotten yourself into, Tank?" Junebug continued to watch as Tank's mouth and head moved in rhythm as he told whatever it was he knew to the captain. "That nigga must be in some deep shit," said Junebug. "His mouth haven't stopped moving for damn near thirty minutes."

After about another fifteen minutes went by of watching Tank, Junebug no longer wanted to let him know he was still back there, so he walked from the door and sat on his bunk. "That nigga is up to no good. I can feel it. Whatever his ass has done, he is in there trying to talk himself out of it," said Junebug in a low whisper as he lay down and looked up at the picture hanging from the top bunk. "I love you, my wonderful Lisa. You was, is, and will always be my world."

***

"I'm here to determine if you need to stay back here in Ad Seg or if I can release you back to general population," said the captain. "Either way is going to really be up to you."

"I didn't do anything," said Tank in a matter-of-fact kind of voice.

"Okay, so I see how this will go," said the captain. "If you don't want to help yourself, then I will watch as you go down with Johnson for capital murder on a police officer, which, I might add, carries the death penalty."

Tank felt a chill go down his back after the captain spoke. "I didn't do anything," said Tank but now with a nervous tone to his voice.

"I won't let you waste any more of my time then," said the captain, and he began to write on the lockup order paper.

Tank started looking around as if he was searching for a way out. Then the look of "I'm trapped" came over his face. "Wait," said Tank. "What is it you want to know?"

The captain, now knowing he had Tank on the hook, said, "Look, I see that you have a release date coming within the next year or so, and I know you want to make it, right?"

Tank didn't respond to the question. He just sat in the chair with his head down.

"Am I right?" yelled the captain, which made Tank jump.

"Yeah," Tank mumbled like a little child.

"I'm sorry. I can't hear you," said the captain, who now smelled blood.

"Yeah, I have a date, and I want to make it," Tank spoke up.

"And what would you do to make that date?" asked the captain, now going in for the kill.

"Anything," answered Tank as he looked the captain in the eye.

"Now that was a very smart answer," said the captain with a smile, knowing he had just made Tank his bitch. "So do you want to tell me how you and your homie from the same gang ended up out together when a c/o was killed, or would you like for me to fill in the blanks with my own version? Keep in mind that I have a remarkable imagination."

*Fuck*, thought Tank. *If I enter this door, ain't no coming back, but then again, if I let these muthafuckas close the door on me by giving me life for this shit, it won't be no coming back from that either.* "Can you guarantee I'll be protected once I tell you all I know?" asked Tank.

"I will do all I can to keep you safe, and I'll talk with the DA on your behalf" said the captain, "but you know there's only one place where I can protect you. Are you ready to go there?"

"So I will be going to SNY," said Tank to himself, and he shook his head, but the word "Okay" came out of his mouth.

"I will need you to sign a few waivers," said the captain. "One will state that you fear for your life in general population. The other ones will say that you don't wish for an attorney to be present as you tell your side of what you saw happen to the officer and that what you are saying is the truth."

"Okay, I'll do it," said Tank.

"We won't need to write your statement," said the captain. "We will record it on tape."

"Can I get your part of the deal on tape as well?" asked Tank.

"Of course, you can," said the captain as he pulled out the recorder and turned it on. "You can begin when you're ready."

It took Tank two hours and seventeen minutes to give his statement. He told him about how everything had gotten started, beginning with how Junebug had jumped the gun and assaulted the officer to how Cdog and only Cdog wanted revenge on the c/os for beating Junebug's ass. Tank even stated on tape five times that he was on the yard that day with Cdog to only talk him out of attacking the staff but that Cdog had threatened to have him and his family killed if he got in the way.

"If it's not too late, you can have someone check the officer's panic button for my fingerprint. I'm the one who pushed it," Tank said, "but that's all I know." He dropped his head.

The captain then stated the terms he had made with Tank and then turned the recorder off. "You made the right choice," said the captain as he put the tape in his pocket. "I will begin the paperwork to have you moved once I can verify your story. However, it's the warden who has the last word on these kinds of cases."

"If you don't think what I just told you is the truth, then have the officer pull my photo album from my property, and behind the fourth picture from the front, they will find a kite from Johnson to me with his plans to assault your officers," said Tank.

"Thank you, and I'll have them get it," said the captain.

"Let's go," said the c/o as he lifted Tank up from the chair.

Tank stepped out of the office and thought to himself, *There's two kinds of people in the world.* He walked back to his cell. *Those who are free and those who are locked up. Ima be free. Fuck all that other shit.*

\*\*\*

Cdog stood in the middle of the hospital room and watched as the two c/os put cuffs around his ankles.

"Raise your arms above your head," said the third c/o from behind Cdog. *These muthafuckas talk all that shit, but look how scary these fools are,* thought Cdog as he raised his arm so the chain could be wrapped around his waist. Cdog turned his head toward the door and caught the eye of one of the two hospital cops who were both armed.

"Give me a reason," said the cop as he put his hand on his hip next to his gun.

Cdog continued to stare at him and smiled. The c/o who was putting the waist chain around Cdog saw the smile and decided to wipe it off Cdog's face by pulling the waist chain as tight as he could get it. Cdog dropped his hands to his waist and tried to loosen the chain up, but before he could, the c/os took him to the floor.

"What are you trying to do?" barked one of the c/os.

"Put your fuckin' hands behind your back," ordered the c/o who was sitting on Cdog's back.

Cdog put his hands where the c/o had told him, but still, he twisted Cdog's arms until they almost broke. Cdog screamed out in pain, which caught the attention of a nurse who ran into the room.

"Aye, is everything all right?" the nurse asked the hospital cop.

"Yeah, it is okay. He just acting like an ass," said one of the c/os.

"Or he may just be in pain from being roughed up right now. Plus, he just had a major operation," said the nurse with a concerned voice.

The c/os realized that the nurse wasn't on their side, so they cuffed Cdog and stood him back up.

"Are you okay?" the nurse asked Cdog, who nodded. "Okay. We will be sending our recommendation to the prison with you on what medication you should have." The nurse looked at all the c/os one by one before walking out of the room.

Cdog was sat on the bed, and the c/os double-checked the locks of the hand and ankle cuffs.

"Let's see if the paperwork is done so we can get the fuck away from this place," said one of the c/os.

Cdog watched as all the officers stepped out into the hall. *Yeah, bitches. Go get the paperwork. I'm ready to shake this shit also. The c/os haven't done nothing but disrespected me since I got here, and being chained to the bed denied me the opportunity to do anything. They think they dealing with a mark*, thought Cdog to himself. *Didn't I already prove to them I'm not the one to fuck over?*

"You can get comfortable," said a c/o, interrupting Cdog's thoughts. "It'll be another hour or so before the paperwork is done."

Cdog made a motion with his cuffed hands as if to say, "What about these?"

The c/o caught what Cdog was saying and shook his head. "We already decided to leave you cuffed and ready to go," said the c/o. "Plus, we don't need another one of your attempts at assaulting one of us." He smiled.

Cdog just stared at him, but that was all it took to make the c/o feel uncomfortable enough to back toward the door.

"If you need to use the restroom, feel free to do so, but just know it's your ass that will be wet or shitty on your ride home."

This comment made all the c/os laugh as they stepped back into the hall.

Cdog sat on the bed and shook his head back and forth. *Your ass gon be wet if I ever get the chance to put my hands on you*, thought Cdog as he closed his eyes to keep his tears from falling out of anger.

Suddenly, his mother's voice took over his mind, and he heard her say her favorite saying: "When people do you wrong, just give it to God."

Cdog opened his eyes and thought, *Not in hell, Momma. Not in hell.*

*** 

"Girl, I know damn well you ain't going back out tonight," said Nesha to Lisa. "This makes the fifth time this week, and you was gone all night on two of the five."

"Bitch, stay out my business. Just be happy I'm doing what I'm doing because it's keeping food in our bellies and the lights on," said Lisa.

"I'm just saying something because I be up all fuckin' night worried about your ass, Lisa. Shit, there's some crazy muthafuckas out there," Nesha said, trying to convince her sister to take a break tonight.

"Look, little sis. In a few months, Tank will be home, and the shit we worry about now won't be a worry then. Trust me on that, but until then, I got to get out there and make a dollar," replied Lisa, who stood up and then flopped back down just as quickly from becoming lightheaded.

What had just happened didn't go unnoticed by Nesha. "Look at you, sis. You can barely stand up, and I won't even comment on your weight loss," said Nesha.

"I know I lost a pound or two, but ain't nothing wrong with me that a good meal and some rest won't fix, but right now, I don't have the time for either," said Lisa.

"Okay," Nesha said in a mocking kind of voice. "You keep saying 'When Tank come home' this and 'Tank come home' that, but what you gon' do when that nigga see how bad you look and move his ass to the next bitch?"

Lisa had no answer for her sister because she had just asked herself that same question yesterday while looking in the mirror. "After tonight, I promise to get some rest," said Lisa, "and I'll go see a doctor if I have to about my weight loss and lack of energy."

"I already lost Momma, Lisa, and I don't wanna go through that shit again with you. That shit hurt, sis, so please, in honor of Momma, get yourself together," Nesha said, and she began to cry.

"I told you Ima get right!" yelled Lisa, now sounding mad. "I'll be back later. Please keep an eye on my baby." She said as she stormed out of the house and slammed the door. Lisa sat on the porch and began to cry as she went down memory lane and thought about how her mom had died at the hands of a trick. "Tank, I need you home now," she mumbled to herself.

Her cellphone began to ring. She looked at the incoming number and knew it was her first date of the night calling. Lisa wiped the tears from her face and cleared her throat. She then hit the answer button on her phone and greeted the caller with a sexy voice. "Hello, Big Poppa."

"I'm about four blocks from your house," came the voice from the other end.

"I'm outside now," said Lisa, and she hung up her phone, pulled out her mirror, and fixed her makeup. "Time to make this money," she said to herself just as the car pulled up to the curb and its driver blew the horn. Lisa walked to the car and got in, not even noticing that the horn had brought Nesha to the front window.

"What the fuck you doing, Lisa?" Nesha asked herself as she saw Lil Cdog's father's car pull off with Lisa in it.

*** Cdog sat in the van and couldn't believe that he was happy to finally be back at the prison. His stay in the hospital was something he wanted to leave in the past. Cdog watched as the razor wire gate opened and the van pulled forward. The gun tower lowered a bucket to the c/o, who got out of the van and reached inside for the keys to the gun shed. The c/o returned to the van, and the driver handed him his handgun. The c/o then walked to the back of the van, where he grabbed a Mini-14 rifle along with a twelve-gauge shotgun. He took all the weapons to the shed. Cdog watched all this with no expression on his face because he had seen this routine numerous times. After putting up the weapons, the c/o hopped back into the van, and the gun tower opened the gate leading into the prison. *Take all this in*, thought Cdog, knowing this would be his last trip anywhere for a while.

Cdog was so caught up in his thoughts, he hadn't noticed that the van had pulled up to the back of Ad Seg. The c/o slamming the door snapped Cdog back to reality really quickly. The c/o disappeared into the building, and what seemed to be two minutes later, seven c/os came back out with him. The driver of the van got out and walked to the side door and opened it. Cdog watched as one of the c/os unlocked the gate to what looked like a kennel.

"Step your ass out," said the driver.

For a brief moment, Cdog's legs wouldn't move out of fear of what was about to happen.

"Move!" yelled the same c/o.

Cdog began to scoot toward the door until his feet landed on top of the footstool. As Cdog stepped out of the van, two c/os grabbed him on both his sides and guided him toward the open cage. One of the c/os began to go into their speech of Ad Seg rules, which Cdog paid no attention to. The cage gate closed, and Cdog was ordered to back up to the slot so the waist chain and handcuffs could be removed.

"Okay, I only want to do this once," said one of the c/os. "Remove all your clothes and put them through the slot."

Cdog began to undress and handed his clothes to the c/o. Once naked, Cdog was ordered to do numerous other things that included bending at the waist and spreading his ass cheeks apart while the c/os looked up his ass for any signs that he had stuck something up there while at the hospital.

"Stay like that until I say otherwise," said the c/o.

Cdog stayed bent over at the waist with both his cheeks spread, but after a couple of seconds, Cdog stood straight up and turned around to face the c/os.

"Oh, so it's true you don't know how to follow orders," said a c/o. "Now you will stay out here naked until you can."

All the c/os then turned and walked back into the building.

Cdog stood in the middle of the cage for what seemed like an hour before he heard keys. Cdog looked toward the door and saw the c/os walking out his way. As they made it to the slot in the gate, one c/o threw a pair of boxers into the cage and ordered Cdog to put them on. He then told Cdog to back up to the slot and place his hands out. When he did, Cdog immediately felt the cold steel cuffs being slammed onto his wrists. Once the cuffs were secure, Cdog heard the lock to the gate turn, and the door was pulled open. Cdog was then ordered to back out to the c/os, who grabbed his arms on both sides when he did.

"Oh yeah, you gonna love your stay here," said one of the c/os with a laugh.

Cdog continued to look forward as he was being guided into the door of the building.

"Incoming!" was being yelled by the other inmates as Cdog was led in.

*So this is the belly of hell*, thought Cdog as he ran his eyes around the building, *and all these fools standing at their door are turds just waiting to be shitted out.*

"When you step inside the cell, continue to face forward," said a c/o.

Cdog stepped into the cell and did as instructed.

He heard the c/o yell, "Close 121!" which the tower did.

"Back up and stick your hands out so we can remove the cuffs," said a c/o.

A half minute later and uncuffed, Cdog found himself alone. He unrolled the bedroll, turned off the light, and lay down. *I'll clean this muthafucka up later*, thought Cdog as he looked around. "Home sweet home," he wanted to say. Cdog closed his eyes and went to sleep.

Cdog was awakened by the sound of the tray slots being slammed as the c/os passed out dinner. *Damn, I must've been tired*, thought Cdog as he got up off the bunk to walk to the door.

"Lights on if you want to eat!" yelled a c/o about three cells down the tier.

Cdog stood at his door window and took in as much of the building as he could. *I wonder where Tank at.* He asked himself as he looked from one cell to the next. The food cart being rolled in front of his door snapped him out of his thoughts.

"Here's your dinner," said a c/o with a smile as handed Cdog three cartons of liquid food. "Enjoy." He slammed the tray slot closed.

Cdog walked back to his bunk and sat down. *I better get used to this shit now*, he thought as he opened one of the cartons. *Damn, this shit nasty as fuck, but I need to put some energy in my body.* Without thinking of the taste, Cdog finished two cartons and then decided to put the third one up for later. He walked back to his door, and once again, the question of where Tank was came back to his mind. He had never even thought about Junebug as he walked back to his bunk and lay down. He picked up the book that was in the cell when he got there and began reading.

\*\*\* Junebug had only seen the back of the dude's head they had brought in earlier. *But that was that nigga Cdog*, thought Junebug. *I wonder what cell they put him in. First Tank, and now, a month later, Cdog come back here.*

*What the fuck these niggas got going on? I need to find out what cell they put him and Tank in.*

Junebug climbed up to his vent. "Excuse me, Cyclone!" yelled Junebug. "Aye, top of the evening," replied Cyclone.

"Back at you," said Junebug. "I need you to do me a favor, if possible."

"What is it, my boy?" asked Cyclone.

"A dude came in earlier, and I think it could be my homie Cdog. Can you find out if it's him? And I need to know what section they got Tank in," asked Junebug.

"Give me about an hour or so, and I should be able to tell you something," said Cyclone.

"Thank you, fool, and you have a solid night," replied Junebug.

"You do the same, my boy," Cyclone said.

Junebug stepped down from the vent and walked to his bunk. "I guess I'll read a few pages of this book," Junebug said, "and wait for the boy to holla at me."

About three hours later, still reading his book, Junebug heard his name being yelled by Cyclone.

"Aye, what it do, my boy?" asked Junebug as he climbed to his vent.

"So trip, fool. I got some info for you," said Cyclone. "The black dude that came earlier ain't answering when my homie call down to him, but they will try again later. Now this next info even fucked me up because I know Tank, but my people said he all bad. He went SNY."

"Damn," replied Junebug. "Are they sure about Tank?"

"It's confirmed. They saw the counselor at his door with the paperwork," said Cyclone.

"Yeah, that will do it for him," said Junebug while shaking his head. "Good looking out, and let me know if they get in touch with the other dude. Y'all have a good night up there."

"I will let you know as soon as I hear something," said Cyclone. "You have a good night as well."

"Yep," said Junebug.

He was about to step down from the vent when Cyclone yelled, "Aye! My cellie want to know if you heard when you will be leaving because he got his endorsement paper and it's to the same SHU as you."

"Naw, I haven't heard nothing, but from what I see, they get muthafuckas outta here in less than a month once you get that ticket," replied Junebug.

"Okay, fo' sho', my boy. Holla if you need me for anything," said Cyclone.

"Likewise," said Junebug as he climbed down from the vent and walked back to his bunk. "Mark-ass nigga. I knew you wasn't built like that," Junebug said to himself about Tank. "Niggas stay claiming they the devil, but when they get to hell, they do whatever to get to heaven."

Junebug burst out laughing. He laughed until tears came from his eyes, but then he realized that his tears weren't tears of something funny. They were tears of frustration from being loyal to niggas who didn't deserve his loyalty, which resulted in him doing life in hell.

"Fuck it," said Junebug. "Ima keep my shit one hundred and live in this hell I created for myself because unlike you, Tank, I am a devil." This statement made him laugh again as he lay on his bunk and picked up his book.

Junebug never found out if that really was Cdog he had seen back there because the very next morning, at four thirty, Junebug was on the bus to the SHU.

*** After being in Ad Seg for twelve days and not having a forty-eight-hour captain hearing, Cdog was taken out of his cell to attend committee. Still unable to talk, Cdog could only listen to the shit they were saying.

"These are some very serious charges over your head," said the warden, who looked at Cdog with hate and anger. "I'm going to clear you for yard and visits but no property."

"We also ask that Inmate Johnson remain on single-cell status," said the captain.

"Single-cell status confirmed," stated the warden as he wrote on a sheet of paper. "Has the incident report been written?"

"Yes, and we were just waiting on Mr. Johnson to return to serve him his copy," answered the lieutenant from the ISU squad. "The DA has already informed us that they will be picking this up and possibly making this a death penalty case."

Everyone in the room looked at Cdog after hearing "death penalty" to see his reaction, but Cdog showed no emotion at all.

"Okay," said the warden, snapping everybody out of the trance they were in. "There's nothing else to discuss here. We will bring you back to committee in sixty days for a status review. Do you understand all that's been said?" asked the Warden.

Cdog nodded.

"Good luck to you, Mr. Johnson," stated the warden as two c/os lifted Cdog out of the chair and escorted him back to his cell.

Cdog sat on his bunk and thought about what the squad lieutenant had said. "Charges will be filed." *Here I am, fighting hard as fuck to come from under one murder case just to face another one. They gon' fuck over me for sure this time,* thought Cdog as he lay down on his bunk and closed his eyes. *They left me some wiggle room for an appeal on the first murder charge, but I'm dead bang on this in-house case. What the fuck was I thinking? I allowed myself to get caught up in these prison politics.*

A loud bang on the wall snapped Cdog out of his thoughts.

"Aye, black in cell 121," the dude said thru the vent.

Cdog stood up and walked to his cell door.

"Aye, black in cell 121!" the dude yelled again.

Cdog went to his desk and grabbed his pencil and paper.

"Aye, this your neighbor in 120," he said in the vent.

*I know where you at,* thought Cdog as he began to strike the dude a kite:

> *Top of the day to you. First, let me say I can't holla back because my jaw is wired, but they call me Cdog. I came from D-yard. I'm active. Are you?*

Cdog ended the kite with that question and folded it up. He then pulled some string from his boxers and made a fishing line. Cdog tied the kite to the line and then slung it until it landed under cell 120. Cdog felt the line being pulled and knew his neighbor had the kite.

A few seconds later, the dude yelled in the vent, "Aye! Okay, homie. My bad. I didn't know about your jaw, but they call me Dreamer, and yeah, I'm active. I was on D-yard myself in Block 2. My homie down the tier named Cyclone asked me to hit you up like almost two weeks ago for the black dude named Junebug."

As soon as Cdog heard the Mexican say Junebug's name, he started a new kite:

> *Okay. Nice to meet you, Dreamer. What cell is my homie Junebug in, and can you get a kite to him? Do you know where they got my homie Tank back here?*

Cdog tied the kite to the line. Then he hit the wall twice to let Dreamer know to pull, which he did. Cdog stood up from the floor and got up to the vent, waiting on Dreamer to reply. It seemed like it took forever before the fool finally said something.

"Junebug got sent to the SHU about a week ago, and as far as that fool Tank, he all bad, my boy. They got him over in the high-risk SNY section," said Dreamer. "He gotta be telling them some real and valid shit to be over there."

Cdog couldn't believe what he was hearing and went back to his pencil and paper.

*You might have the wrong person,* Cdog wrote. *Are you sure the dude you speaking about is my homie Tank?*

Cdog folded the kite and tied it to the line. He then hit the wall twice. Dreamer pulled the line in, and Cdog stood up and looked out his cell door toward the corner of the building but couldn't see because of the stairs blocking his view.

"Oh yeah, I'm sure it's Tank. We both had jobs on the yard crew," said Dreamer.

*Damn,* thought Cdog as he stared at the vent. *This shit starting to make sense now. That nigga set me up from the start.*

"Aye, Cdog, I won't hold you up any longer due to your jaw and shit, so you have a good day, and if I can assist you with anything, just knock on the wall," said Dreamer.

Cdog hit the vent twice with his hand and bent down to pull his line back in. *That nigga Tank,* thought Cdog as he lay back on his bunk. *Junebug was right about him all this time. The nigga is a straight ho.* Cdog closed his eyes, and the first thought that came to his mind was *Ain't gon' be no wiggle room on this one. I'm dead. Bang.*

***

After being situated in the SHU for two weeks, Junebug decided to write Lisa a letter, pouring out his feelings and confessing his undying love for her. His main reason for the letter was to inform her of the bitch-ass nigga Tank. Junebug actually thought that if he showed Lisa what kind of nigga Tank was, she would run back to his arms. Junebug made up a story about how Tank was being fucked by his cellie constantly, and once they, the police, found out, Tank made the decision to go to SNY. He filed charges on his cellie and then told on about nine more niggas. Junebug went on to say that he had heard they no longer called him Tank because he only answered to Tankeisha. Junebug laughed out loud to himself at the name he had given Tank.

"That bitch-ass nigga got more woman in him than you," Junebug continued, "so I hope you make the right choice and come back where you know you belong, which is by my side. I forgive you, Lisa, and want you back in my life, so please, I'm begging you, write me back and say, 'Yes, it's me and you against the world.'"

Junebug went on and on about him and her, and at no time in his letter did he bring up or ask about his daughter. After he finished the letter, he reread it out loud to himself, stopping only to laugh at the name Tankeisha. He folded the letter, filled out the envelope, and placed it in his cell door so the c/o could pick it up at count time.

Thinking that he had just created a work of art, Junebug sat on his bunk and said out loud, "I just gotta wait on her now." He looked at the picture he had of Lisa and smiled at it. "I know you love me, Lisa. You just confused." *Ima get you back right*, thought Junebug, *and Ima pay that bitch-ass nigga Tankeisha back.* The last thought made Junebug go into uncontrollable laughter. "Tankeisha," he said to himself, which seemed to make him laugh even harder. He laughed until tears came from his eyes and his side began to cramp up.

Junebug walked to the sink and pushed the cold water button. Scooping the water into his hands, he splashed it on his face. Then he took a long drink. "I need my fuckin' meds!" he yelled out to no one. He wiped the water from his sink and then looked out his cell door window for a second. He then turned and walked back to his bunk. "Ain't shit to do but lie in this coffin," he said to himself as he lay down. His eyes, on their own, went to the picture on the top bunk. "We gon' get our shit right, Lisa," he whispered to the picture before closing his eyes.

***

"Damn, I wonder what's taking so long to get me where I'm going," Tank asked himself as he paced the floor of his cell. He had been back there going on a month now and had signed all the required papers to be housed at an SNY. "These muthafuckas might be on some slick shit," Tank continued to talk to himself out loud. If they don't have me right by the time they need me to take the stand against Cdog, then I ain't doing the shit."

Panic began to take over his mind as he thought that no matter what, his ass could never go back to the main line. "My career is over," he whispered as he continued to walk in his cell. Then a whole new thought came to his mind. *The same fools I helped get off the yard will now be my neighbors.* "That may be a whole new situation I need to deal with," Tank said. "Man, I ain't got time to be fucking around like that. I'm trying to get home."

Tank stopped walking and sat on his bunk. He thought about how setting up Cdog was what had cemented his release date. *I wasn't gon' do Cdog like that. My plans were for Junebug's dumb ass, but Junebug being Junebug, he did some dumb shit, so I had to revise my plans. Now Cdog is the fall guy. That nigga had the nerve to strike Big Tank a kite, telling me what we gon' do.* "Ain't that a bitch?" Tank said.

*Yeah, I'm sure he will send Big Cdog a letter to let him know what I did, but I already got plans for his bitch ass anyway for knocking down my cousin Hotdog, so yep, Ima enjoy this three-piece meal of Big Cdog, Lil Cdog, and Junebug. Ima lick my fuckin' fingers when I'm done eating. You niggas ain't shit in my eyes,* Tank thought. "Nothing but my victims," he said. "Lil Cdog and Junebug gon' die doing life in this manmade hell, but me? Ima do my life in the real hell, which is on the streets. I'm about to go get that money and fuck plenty of bitches. Ima go home to Lisa, but I can't make her my wife. She ain't shit but a rat."

Tank sat there and daydreamed of the things he had planned once he touched down. "They need to hurry up and process my paperwork so I can get from back here." *I'm in jail, in jail,* thought Tank as he looked around the cell. "Man, Big Tank too fly to be living like this," he said to himself.

His mood quickly became sad when he thought about some lyrics he had heard a few months back while on the yard when a couple of niggas stood around and battled each other. "Free all the niggas. That's real. Kill all the pussy niggas who squeal." Tank lay back on his bunk and remembered when he had thought those lyrics sounded hard as fuck and how now he had become the nigga who needed to be killed. "I don't give a fuck," Tank said to himself. "I'm still a real one." Tank knew that was a lie after he had said it and knew that one day his decision would catch up to him. "Ima be ready for you, niggas!" Tank yelled at the top of his voice.

"Me too!" someone down the tier shouted back.

Tank just smiled as he lay on his bunk. "Ima be ready," he said again but only loud enough for him to hear.

\*\*\*

It had been over a month since Cdog left the hospital, and he was beginning to get some function in his jaw. He still couldn't eat solid food, and although, he could say certain words, it still hurt like crazy for him to talk. Since confirming that Tank was back there with him, Cdog stood at his cell door each and every time they ran yard with hopes of seeing Tank. Cdog refused to rely on the word of a Mexican that Tank went to the SNY. He had come to the conclusion that until he saw Tank with the SNYs or read some paperwork on him, Tank was still good. Cdog was taught when he had first gotten to prison that if it ain't in black and white, then it ain't right. *I have seen some stand-up niggas get knives ran up in them on assumptions or bullshit information.* Plus, he knew that no matter what, he couldn't go off just the word of a Mexican because for one, they hated blacks behind these walls, and two, most Mexicans were snake-ass dope fiends.

Cdog was glad when they had moved his neighbor. He was tired of the fishing line kite game. Plus, he was back on his workout tip, trying to rebuild all the strength he had lost the last couple of months. Between only being on liquid and laid up, he dropped a lot of weight. Cdog knew that it would be about another five to eight weeks before he could even think about eating regular food, so all through the day, he drank water and did pushups.

Cdog hadn't received his write-up yet because a week ago, like most inmates, he had postponed that entire process until after he finished court. He hadn't been charged or read his rights because the case was pending, but he knew it would happen soon. The DA was just crossing all *t*'s and dotting all *i*'s. *Them muthafuckas gon' try to sit my ass on death row for this one*, thought Cdog, which brought his mother's face to his mind. *This is gon' break her heart. How am I going to explain this?* Cdog dropped his head. *I have continued to let the one person who believed in me down. Yeah, this gon' hurt the fuck outta her when she find out.* Cdog dropped down in the pushup position with anger and frustration all over his face.

"I'm sorry, Momma," he whispered to himself as tears ran from his eyes. He began doing pushups and then said one more time, "I'm so sorry, Momma."

***

"Man, I heard them niggas killed a c/o," said Popeye to one of the dudes on the block.

"Yeah, I heard that same shit. My bitch got a brother up there with them fools," said Gino, but he didn't mention what he had heard about Popeye's cousin, Tank.

Gino raised the bottle of Remy to his mouth, trying to ease the thought of what Popeye had asked to do with him tonight. It had been enough time since the murder of Hotdog for Popeye to do what he wanted without raising any suspicion from anyone. The only other person to know his plans was his childhood friend, Gino.

"Ima kill that nigga Big Cdog," Popeye told Gino, "but Ima need your help."

"Shit, what you need me to do?" asked Gino, who was already on team "Fuck Cdog" since he had emptied that clip at Hotdog and hit Gino in the arm.

"Every Thursday night him and that bitch Karen go out to eat. They haven't missed a Thursday since I started stalking the nigga," explained Popeye. "When he drop Karen off, I just need you to be down the street with the hood of your car up. Once the nigga see you, he gon' pull over, and I'll do the rest."

"Fuck that. Ima put a bullet back in his ass," replied Gino. Little did he know that that was what Popeye was banking on from his longtime friend.

"Nigga, slow down on that drink. We gotta bust a move tonight," said Popeye, snapping Gino back to the present.

"I'm good, my boy, just gotta take the edge off," Gino shot back.

"Yeah, alrite. Just don't overdo it," Popeye snapped while looking at his watch. *Man, I've waited a long time for this moment*, thought Popeye. *I knew a couple weeks after Hotdog was killed that Little Cdog didn't do it, but I had to wait this shit out. Muthafuckas tell nowadays just because the police ask a question.*

"Nigga, you worried about how much I'm drinking when you need to be rolling up some of that killa," Gino said as he took a swig.

"No doubt, my boy. I do need to smoke something," said Popeye as he reached into his pocket and pulled out the blunt wrap and weed.

"But back to what I was saying a little while ago," said Gino. "My girl brother said them niggas did the c/o bad."

"Shit, I think Lil Cdog had action on his appeal, and from what my auntie said, Tank is on his way home," stated Popeye as he dumped the weed into the wrap.

"If what you just said is true, then both them niggas gotta be sick," Gino said as he grabbed his stomach.

"Fuck sick. Them niggas might be ready to kill themselves," said Popeye and they both broke out laughing. Popeye put some fire to the blunt and hit it, which made him cough. "Yeah, my boy, this that killa." He passed it to Gino, who took a long pull and coughed as well.

"'Bout time you got killa. You be having that gobba goo so much," said Gino.

That last comment made both of them laugh.

Popeye took a glance at his watch and said, "It's time, fool."

They both got in their own car and drove off. When they were down the street from Karen's house, who lived on a dead-end street, they pulled over.

"Ima park my shit around the corner," Popeye told Gino over his cellphone. "I see the nigga car in her driveway, so he down there."

They stood outside Gino's car, smoking the last of the blunt and looking toward Karen's house. After what felt like two hours, they saw Big Cdog come out of the house and jumped into his car.

"Ima be in the bushes. Don't let that nigga pass you up," said Popeye as he ran to the bushes.

Gino raised the hood of his car, and as Cdog was driving by, Gino raised his head up, just like Popeye said.

Cdog pulled over and jumped out of his car. "Trade this bullshit-ass bucket in and get you something worth driving," said Cdog as he walked toward Gino.

"Fuck you, nigga. Give me the money to buy something," Gino said with a smile.

"What you need? A jump or something?" asked Cdog as he put his head under the hood of Gino's car.

"I don't think so. Just cover that hole," said Gino.

"What hole, nigga?" Cdog asked as he looked around the engine.

"The hole that's gonna be in your head," said Gino as he pulled the .44 from the radiator and shot Cdog in the stomach before he could run or grab for the gun.

Popeye ran from the bushes with his gun out. He stood over Cdog, who was moaning and groaning from the pain of the first shot. "Payback time, you bitch-ass nigga," said Popeye as he shot Cdog in the head twice. "That's for you, big bro. Now you can rest in peace."

Gino slammed the hood of his car down, which snapped Popeye out of the trance he was in. "We gotta get the fuck on," said Gino, who walked to where Cdog lay and shot him one more time in the head to be certain he was dead. Gino knew how dangerous Big Cdog was, and he wasn't taking any chances.

"I'm gone," said Popeye as he ran toward his car around the corner.

"I'm right behind you!" yelled Gino as he jumped in his car.

They pulled off, leaving Cdog dead in the street. Popeye blew his car horn twice at Gino, who did the same. Then they both threw up the Bottoms gang sign at each other and drove off in different directions.

*** 

Three weeks after the murder of Big Cdog, Lil Cdog sat on his bunk and stared at the envelope the c/o had given him at mail call. *This shit gotta be bad news*, thought Cdog. *I been in this muthafucka all this time, and she never wrote to me.* He stared at his sister's name and wondered what bad news she had sent him. Cdog closed his eyes and said a prayer to God, asking for his mother and father to be all right. Then he tore the tape off the envelope and pulled out the contents inside. As soon as he had seen a little of it, he knew it was an obituary.

Cdog put it back inside and said to himself, "I'm not ready for this shit." He lay down, and a million thoughts ran through his mind, but none were pleasant. He thought about how he hadn't heard from his mom in a few months, and in her last letter, she said she wasn't feeling too good. *Please don't let this be you, Momma*, he thought to himself as he grabbed the envelope. This time, he pulled the letter and obituary all the way out.

When he turned it over to the front, his heart skipped a beat as he looked at the photo of Big Cdog. Karen had even written a few lines on a sheet of paper. Cdog read it and couldn't believe what he was reading. He was found dead right down the street from her house with three holes in his head and one in the stomach. "Nobody seen shit" was how she had ended her letter. Cdog's mind went into overdrive because he knew that Big Cdog was too smart and paid too much attention to detail to get caught up slipping by an enemy. This was an in-house hit, and whoever did it was scared shitless of Big Cdog. That was why they had hit him three times in the head. *They knew that nigga would've came for that ass*, thought Lil Cdog. "Damn, my boy, you let them catch you with your pants down," said Cdog.

Looking at the obituary, he no longer had fucked-up feelings for his big homie. Instead, he had feeling of revenge. *Ima find out who did this to you and make them pay if I ever run into them*, Lil Cdog vowed to the picture of his big homie. "Rest in peace, fool," Cdog said, and he held up the peace sign to the photo. He placed the obituary back inside the envelope and lay back on his bunk to remember some of the good moments he had shared with Big Cdog. "RIP, my boy," he whispered before closing his eyes.

*** 

"So how the fuck you think these bills getting paid?" asked Lisa, who was in a heated argument with her sister, Nesha, who wasn't trying to hear Lisa's bullshit.

"Bitch, I'm just saying you doing some straight low shit to get a few punk-ass dollars," Nesha shot back. "You are out all hours of the night, and I'm cooking, cleaning, and watching your daughter like I'm her momma."

Everything Nesha had just said made Lisa drop her head in shame because it was all the truth. She had been out lying on her back more this past month because turning tricks had become her way of revenge. She knew she had some kind of disease but refused to go get a checkup. Instead, she told herself that whatever she had, she was going to pass it to every nigga she could. "I know what you saying, lil sis, and I promise I'm almost finished with this lifestyle," said Lisa. "My Tank will be home soon."

"And everything supposed to go back to normal when he do?" asked Nesha.

"No, they not. I'm just saying I won't have to run and work these streets anymore. We will, however, get the chance to be a family again—a normal one, at least," answered Lisa.

Nesha looked at her sister and shook her head. *Your ass is dying, and you don't even see it*, thought Nesha. "So when are you going to the doctor so you can find out what's wrong with you?" asked Nesha.

"Ima go soon, sis. I promise," lied Lisa, who had no intentions of visiting a doctor. She already felt that the shit eating away at her body was incurable. "Can we just relax right now?" Lisa pulled out a bag of weed, knowing how to shut her pothead sister up.

"Is that some of that killa from Popeye?" asked Nesha. "Because he got it in right now."

"Yeah, this from him," answered Lisa.

"Ima stay off your head for now, but I'm worried about you, sis," said Nesha.

"I'm gon' be all right. Trust and believe me on that. Now let's smoke," said Lisa.

"That part right there," said Nesha, and they both burst out laughing. "So what you think about that letter from Junebug?" asked Nesha, and she looked at her sister, who gave her a frown. "Yeah, bitch, I read your letter. So what?" Nesha said.

"Fuck that nigga Junebug," said Lisa. "I can't wait to let Tank read that shit."

"He said some crazy stuff," said Nesha. Then she asked, "Do you think it's true?"

"That nigga just butthurt 'cause I don't want him," answered Lisa. "Girl, we both know damn well that Tank is a beast."

"Yeah, I feel you, but at the same time, I know that some niggas be a beast on the streets with their guns and shit but turn kitty cat when they hit that yard," said Nesha, and she started laughing.

"Bitch, shut the fuck up," replied Lisa with a smile. *I know my nigga still A1.*

They were both feeling the effect of the weed when Nesha asked, "Girl, what about that name Junebug called Tank?"

"Tankeisha!" they both yelled at the same time as they fell to the floor, holding their stomachs in laughter.

***

"All of your paperwork and whatnot should be all in order within the next two weeks or so," said the counselor to Tank, standing in front of his cell door.

"Why is this taking so long?" asked Tank.

"There's a procedure we must follow in cases like yours," the counselor said. "Your history here raised a few eyebrows when the request for SNY went on by the boss's desk, but now that she has approved it, we are just waiting on the confirmation from the department head, and they move when they want to, not when we ask them to."

"Man, what you just said don't sound like nothing but a stall tactic to be certain Ima take the stand against Johnson. I've already fucked my career off behind these walls. I can never step foot on another main line because of that signed affidavit, but ya'll got me doing a SHU program back here for helping ya'll. I didn't have to do this shit," Tank stated.

"Let's be clear, Mr. Adams. You ain't helping no one but yourself. Now as I stated before, all your paperwork should catch up in the next couple of weeks. I don't have to, but let me advise you of this. If you plan on doing any funny business when it comes to giving your testimony, that warden won't even hesitate feeding you to the lions by putting your ass back in general population. So just relax and let the paperwork catch up. You have a nice day," the counselor said, and he walked off, leaving Tank standing at the door in deep thought of the threat on being forced back to the main line, and it scared the shit out of him.

As Tank began to sit on the toilet, he said to himself, "I'm too far in to turn back now. I got no choice but to see this all the way out. Fuck you, Cdog." Shit began to hit the bottom of his toilet. *At least two more weeks of this shit*, he thought as he looked around the empty cell. "I can do that because my reward gon' be walking outta these gates to freedom," Tank whispered to himself.

*** Cdog sat up on his bunk and looked around his cell. This was the third night in a row that the scene of Hotdog's murder haunted his sleep. He kept seeing Hotdog hit the ground with brain splatter all around him and Popeye yelling that his brother was dead. "What the fuck?" said Cdog as he walked to the sink in his cell and threw water on his face. When he looked into the mirror, the reason why he was being haunted with the nightmares hit him like a ton of bricks. "Popeye," Cdog whispered as he continued to look in the mirror. "That's who did that shit to Big Cdog," he said out loud to himself.

He dried his face and sat on his bunk in thought. *Everybody in the bottom knew I didn't kill Hotdog, and Popeye played the waiting game to seek his revenge.* "Damn, it all makes perfect sense," Cdog whispered as he reached inside his locker and pulled out the obituary of Big Cdog. He began to frown at the picture looking back at him. "You taught me this shit, so how the fuck did you allow that nigga Popeye to outthink you?" Cdog asked in a low voice. "'Pay attention, and always know who you at war with.' That's what you taught me, my nigga."

Tears rolled down his face, which was the first time he had cried for Big Cdog since receiving his obituary. "Don't trip, my boy. I got you. That fool gon' pay, and I promise you that." He put the obituary back into his locker. Cdog lay down and closed his eyes but knew sleep wasn't an option because his heart was beating to the rhythm of revenge. "I just can't seem to shake the demons of trouble," Cdog said as he stared at the top bunk.

Cdog had fallen back to sleep and was jolted awake by the knocking on his cell door. *Damn, I was out*, thought Cdog as he got out of bed and walked to the door.

"Mr. Johnson, today the doctor will be calling you in to see about removing the wire from your jaw," said the nurse, who was standing in front of Cdog's cell with a c/o.

"Okay," said Cdog as he held his hand out to receive his medication.

The nurse and c/o watched like hawks as he took it.

"It'll be two or three hours after you eat breakfast," the nurse said as she moved to the next cell.

*Yes*, thought Cdog as he looked in the mirror. "This shit coming off today," he mumbled to himself and then smiled. He walked to his bunk and waited for them to pass out breakfast. "Let's get this shit going," he said as he lay back down.

Not even five minutes later, Cdog heard the c/o yelling, "Open cell 124!"

Hearing the panic in his voice made Cdog get up and walk to his door and look down the tier toward 124.

"Get your ass on the ground now!" barked a c/o. "Open the door!" he yelled at the tower.

Unable to see clearly to 124, Cdog stood at his door and waited. He heard the door being opened and a c/o telling someone they had better not move.

"Close it!" the c/o yelled out to the tower.

Cdog heard the door slam shut. What he saw next made his stomach turn. Two c/os were dragging a Mexican along the floor by the arms. He was going into convulsions. They let him go right in front of Cdog's cell, and that was when Cdog saw the split down the right side of the dude's face caused by some razors. The gash was from his temple to his chin, and as Cdog looked harder, he saw blood shooting in the air from the dude's neck, where another gash ran from one side to the other side. Blood was all over the floor in front of Cdog's cell. *Damn, my cellie tore his ass up*, thought Cdog as he watched the dude body's shake. The c/os did nothing but stand and watch as they waited for medical to arrive. *Even the gatekeepers watch you die in hell*, thought Cdog as he looked at the c/os.

Finally, two nurses got there and went to work wrapping the dude up in bandages. The medical wagon was let in the building through the back door. They rolled the cart in and loaded the Mexican on it, and he was gone. The c/os then focused their attention back on cell 124.

"Lie on the floor," one of them ordered.

Cdog had seen enough for the morning and walked back to his bunk. "Damn, the things you see when you doing life in hell, and all this shit happened before breakfast." The last statement made Cdog shake his head and chuckle. He didn't even get up to see who they had brought out of cell 124 because to him, it didn't matter. *The Mexicans can kill one another all they want. That's just one less muthafucka to deal with when shit kick off between us*, thought Cdog. "Fuck 'em!" he yelled from his bunk, looking toward the door.

*** It had been eight days since Tank spoke to that counselor, and he was counting down every day. *The only excitement so far was when that shit happened at cell 124*, thought Tank. All the other days felt like being alive in a walk-in grave. There was nothing to do or no one to talk to. "All I do is lie in this coffin," Tank said as he looked at the bed hanging from the wall.

*Man, I didn't realize how bad this prison shit was until I came back here*, thought Tank. *This entire system is nothing but a manmade hell. I can't wait to be home and put all this behind me.* "They ain't gonna have to worry about the Tank again," he said while mentally vowing to never return to prison once they freed him. *I'm holding court in the streets starting from the first day of my release all the way until*, thought Tank. *I prefer death to this shit right here.* "That stupid-ass nigga had the nerve to say in his rap that he rather be judged by twelve than carried by six," Tank said to himself. "Your ass saying that because you ain't been through this shit, and it sounded good."

Tank walked to his bunk and lay down in deep thought of freedom. *They need to get me to where they sending me so I can start making a few moves to stack me some paper I can go home with. I already got the bitch Lisa ready to play her part and bring me the sack. Plus, the police that was moving cans of tobacco is working on the SNY yard, so I need to holla at him and see if he still fucking around.* Tank smiled as he thought about how he had everything planned out. "Muthafuckas can't outthink the Tank," he said. "Ima be all right." Tank rolled on his side and stared at the wall. *Ima be all right,* he thought as he closed his eyes.

About two hours later, Tank was woken up by a knock on his cell door.

"Adams, I got some mail for you," said the c/o as he slid it through the side of the door.

Tank grabbed the envelope and walked back to his bunk. He opened the envelope, and inside was a copy of all the paperwork he had signed for the SNY process. His eyes finally ran across the copy of the approval. Tank smiled. "About damn time," he said. "I'm out this bitch." Now all he had to do was wait on a bed, and from what he had noticed, that only took up to three, maybe four days after receiving your papers. "Y'all can have this shit," Tank said to himself, looking around the cell. Then he reread the paper of approval.

***

"Aye, Johnson, get ready," said the c/o as he shoved a jumpsuit through the tray slot. "Some people up front need to see you."

*What the fuck could this be about?* thought Cdog as he grabbed the jumpsuit. Once dressed, he went through the process of having the waist chain put on him. After the c/o secured his hands in the cuffs, he yelled to the tower to open cell 122. The door began to open, and almost immediately, Cdog felt hands grabbing him. The c/os escorted him to a chair and told him to place his knees on it, after which they put ankle cuffs on him. Cdog was then taken out the back door to a waiting van that, not even a half minute later, pulled in front of RR, which was where inmates were processed for release or received into the prison. Cdog was pulled out of the van and placed inside a holding tank in RR.

The c/o removed Cdog's hands from the cuffs but left on the waist and ankle chains. "They should be here soon," said the c/o, and he walked away from the tank.

*What the fuck is this about?* Cdog asked himself as he sat down on the concrete bench. *And who the fuck is they?* He heard the door open, and both of Cdog's questions were answered as he saw two detectives walk in with two squad c/os, straight to the tank, and one of them pulled out a card and fingerprint ink.

"We need to take your prints," the officer said, and then he asked Cdog to state his full name, date of birth, and prison ID number. Once he verified the info, he began the fingerprint process. "Any questions or comments can be directed at them," said the squad c/o as he pointed to the detectives.

Cdog finished up with the fingerprints and was cleaning his hands when the detectives walked to the tank.

"I'm Detective Murray, and this is Detective Scott," said the tall red-faced one.

"Before we go any further, let me advise you of your rights," said the short fat one, who then went into the Miranda spill. When he was done, he asked Cdog if he understood what he had just said.

"Yeah, I do," shot Cdog.

"Okay," said Murray. "The state has formally charged you with first-degree capital murder, which makes this case eligible for the death penalty." Murray paused to let that last part sink in before he continued. "At this time, would you like to give us your version of what happened?"

"I have nothing to say," replied Cdog.

"Look, Johnson, this is your one chance to help yourself," said Scott.

"I have nothing to say," replied Cdog once again.

"Okay, Mr. I-Have-Nothing-to-Say, but off the record, your homie Adams, a.k.a. Tank, had a lot to say, and none was in your favor," Murray chimed in.

"I have nothing to say," replied Cdog for the third time, but now he was thinking that it was all true, what the Mexican had told him about Tank.

Detective Murray shook his head and leaned into the bars of the tank and whispered, "I'll be there when they have your ass strapped to the table and push that deadly needle into your arm, and I'll see then if you have nothing to say." He smiled at Cdog as he turned from the bars and walked away.

On cue, like a movie scene, Scott spoke up. "Come on, Mr. Johnson. We're trying to help you. Regardless of what my partner just told you, I don't want to see a needle pushed in your arm."

*Look at these dumb muthafuckas*, thought Cdog. *They playing good cop, bad cop.* "I have nothing to say," replied Cdog. Detective Murray walked back to the bars, and for the next forty-five minutes, both the detectives fired a series of questions at Cdog, whose answer for each question remained the same.

Finally fed up, the detectives turned to the c/os and said, "We are done here."

Cdog was taken back to his cell. Sitting on his bunk, he couldn't think of anything but being executed. *I'm dead bang for sure on this one*, thought Cdog, and it made his stomach turn. He jumped off his bunk and ran to the toilet, where he threw up until he had nothing left inside him.

***

Junebug stood at the door of his cell and waited for the c/o to walk past, with hopes that today would be the day he heard back from Lisa.

"I got something for you today," said the c/o as he slid the mail through the side of the door.

Junebug's heart began to pound in his chest at a rapid beat. *Please let this be what I wish for*, thought Junebug as he grabbed for the mail and pulled it all the way into his cell. He instantly felt anger and disappointment. "Aye, fuck you!" Junebug yelled at the c/o, who was three doors down from his cell.

The c/o turned toward Junebug and smiled before moving down the tier.

"Fuck Ima do with this?" Junebug asked himself, looking at the medical chromo in his hand. He balled the paper up and threw it in the toilet. *She didn't get my letter*, thought Junebug, which had become his excuse for her every time he had written her and didn't receive a reply.

In fact, the only person to respond to his letters was his little brother. He was the one who had told him about Big Cdog, but he couldn't send an obituary because they only gave them to a few people. His little bro also kept him informed on the family. Junebug sat on his bunk as he realized that without the info coming from his brother, he would be cut the fuck off from anything and everyone he loved on the outside. *Damn, I know I made some mistakes and fucked-up decisions*, thought Junebug, *but do I really deserve to be treated like this?* "Fuck naw," he said. "As much shit as I did for my family, ain't no way I should be going through the things I do." *They don't owe me nothing, and my actions put me in prison, but out of love, if our paths ever cross again, they gon' have to explain this shit*, Junebug thought. "I even got the bitch-ass c/os clowning me." June shook his head in disgust. "Yeah, they gon' have to explain this shit." Junebug lay down. His eyes, like clockwork, went straight to the photo of Lisa hanging from the top bunk. "I love you too," he said to the photo as if it had spoken to him first. "I will always love you, Lisa."

***

Three days after seeing the detectives, Cdog was escorted to the visiting room for a visit with a lawyer. Cdog sat behind the glass window and stared at his court-appointed attorney.

"Today I'm just here to introduce myself and go over the charges with you. My name is Jerome Cooper. I have practiced law for the last twenty-seven years, in which time I've worked on about eight cases that were death penalty eligible. The court, at any time, could decide to take me off your case. That won't be up to me, but that's how it goes when you don't pay for your own attorney," Cooper said without taking a breath. "These charges, they come, so we don't have room to play around. They will be bringing you to court on Tuesday, and at that time, the judge will officially charge you and ask how you plead."

Cdog shot the lawyer a look that said, "If this glass wasn't here, I would slap the shit out of you," but he answered, "Not guilty."

There was a slight pause before Cooper said, "Okay, so that's what we will enter."

"Out of the eight cases, how many of them went to death row?" asked Cdog.

Cooper looked Cdog in the eye, and with confidence, he said, "One. I'm very good at what I do, and what I do is keep people, who may even deserve it, off death row."

"So what you think you can do on my case?" asked Cdog, suddenly feeling like he had a chance.

"Too soon to tell. I haven't read all the paperwork yet," said Cooper as he began to put things back into his briefcase, signaling to Cdog that this meeting was about over. "If there's no more questions, then I'll see you on Tuesday."

"Naw, I don't have any questions," replied Cdog as he watched Cooper gather his things to leave.

Three days later, Cdog stood in front of the judge and entered a not-guilty plea to all charges. A court date was set for a preliminary hearing, and Cdog was ushered out of the courtroom and into a waiting van.

\*\*\*

Tank sat on his bunk and was hotter than some fish grease. *Everybody I seen so far that got their paper of approval for SNY was gone within four days, but here it is, day eight, and I'm still the fuck back here*, thought Tank. He got up off his bunk and walked to the door. He stared down at the c/os just sitting around at the police podium, getting paid for doing nothing.

"Aye, c/o! I need to talk to someone!" Tank yelled out the side of his door.

None of the c/os moved or even looked his way, which made Tank even hotter.

"Aye, muthafuckas! I know ya'll can hear me!" Tank yelled.

Still, the c/os didn't respond, so Tank began kicking the door. He kicked it so hard that it almost went off track.

"Stop kicking the fucking door!" one of the c/os hollered, but none of them got out of their chairs to come up to his cell, so he started kicking the door again, this time nonstop, until finally, a c/o popped up at his door.

"What the fuck is your problem, you fucking asshole?" the c/o asked.

"I need to talk to someone about why I'm still back here," Tank said, out of breath from kicking the door.

"And you think making all this noise will get you outta here sooner?" asked the c/o.

"Man, I yelled down there, but you muthafuckas acted like ya'll didn't hear me," shot Tank.

"Look," said the c/o, "when it's your turn to leave, you will leave, but until then, you need to sit your ass down and wait. Nobody here move when you want them to, so you can stop with all that kicking and yelling."

"Can I speak to a sergeant or somebody with some rank?" asked Tank.

"The sergeant is busy and don't got time to be dealing with your bullshit. I just told your ass you don't run nothing around here, which mean no one has to move when you say so, but I'll tell you who would love to deal with you," said the c/o as he got to the crack of Tank's door, and he began to whisper, "Mr. Johnson down there in cell 121 would probably love to have you as his cellmate." The c/o started laughing and turned to walk away. "And stay the fuck off the door!" he yelled at Tank over his shoulder.

"Bring me a complaint form" was all Tank could say as he watched the c/o walk back downstairs. Tank stood at the door and could barely see cell 121. "So that's where you are," mumbled Tank. "I wish I could've seen the look on your face when you found out it was me who fucked over you."

*What you thought, nigga? That you got away with disrespecting me by fucking my bitch and disrespecting my family by driving off with Big Cdog after he killed my cousin? Naw, nigga. You don't play the Tank like that. I'm looking forward to getting on the stand against your ass,* thought Tank. *You ain't shit in this game, Cdog. You just the nobody nigga that took the somebody-nigga case. You ain't done shit else for the hood. Except kill that c/o.* Tank smiled. *You already got life, so I hope they fry your ass this time. Oh, and me? I'll be walking my black ass up outta here in less than a year.*

"Don't trip, Junebug. I haven't forgot about you. Your turn coming too. Fuck both ya'll niggas," Tank said as he sat down on the toilet to take a dump. "And muthafuckas do move when I tell them to!" he yelled from the toilet toward the cell door. "I'm Big Tank, bitch."

***

Cdog sat in the visiting room and listened to what his lawyer was saying. "I think it would be best to postpone your prelim," said Cooper.

"Why is that?" Cdog asked. "It ain't nothing but a hearing to see if there's enough state evidence for me to stand trial, and we both already know that nine times outta ten, that's what will happen."

Cooper looked at Cdog and found himself respecting the fact that this young dude, although faced with the death penalty, was calm and focused. "You right," Cooper said, "but this is also the hearing where I can attack their evidence so they wouldn't be able to use it at trial."

"Honestly, man, this shit don't really matter to me," said Cdog. "You the lawyer, so go ahead and do what you feel need to be done."

"I don't want to do anything you don't feel all the way comfortable with," said Cooper.

"Naw, for real, go ahead and do you," replied Cdog.

"This delay will give me the chance to look at what they got against you and talk to the DA," stated Cooper.

"Talk to the DA about what?" asked Cdog. Cooper made eye contact with Cdog, trying without words to let him know that he had Cdog's best interest in what he was about to say. "To see if they are willing to strike a deal at some point."

"A deal," commented Cdog with a frown.

"As I told you before, Mr. Johnson, my job is to keep you off death row, and if a plea deal does that, then I've done my job," said Cooper. "I can go into court later today and postpone the prelim hearing without you having to come, if that's okay with you."

"I already told you. Do what you do. I'm good with it," answered Cdog.

"I'll be back in a few days, at which time I should've gone through and read all the paperwork and talked with the DA," said Cooper as he gathered up his things. "Oh yeah, I almost forgot to ask you again. Is there anyone you want or need me to contact?"

"No," Cdog answered quickly. "I don't need or want you to contact anyone for me, and please don't take it upon yourself to contact anyone on my behalf." Cdog then frowned at his lawyer to let him know that he was serious. Cdog didn't want his mom to find out about his situation. He knew it would break her down if she knew he was fighting a death penalty case. She had a heart attack when he was fighting his first case, and the death penalty wasn't even on the table.

"Okay, Mr. Johnson. I hear you loud and clear. I'll do the court appearance today and will see you soon," said Cooper. "You try to have a good day."

"Yep. You do the same," said Cdog.

For the next few days, Cdog kept busy by working out, reading, and finally writing some letters. He still refused to let his mom know about his situation, even though she had asked in her letter if he was involved in an officer being killed.

"I'm in Ad Seg," he told her, "for a riot with the Mexicans, and during the riot, an officer had been hurt bad, but I had nothing to do with that."

Cdog knew that it was his sister telling his mom what the hood was gossiping about. Cdog still hadn't seen Tank and began to wonder if the nigga was actually back there. Cdog's weight and strength were back up, mainly because he did revenge pushups. All he saw in his mind were Tank and the boy Popeye, so to not punch the wall of his cell out of anger, he busted down instead with pushups. *I'll have my hands on one of you niggas soon enough,* thought Cdog, *and I'm not stopping until one of us ain't breathing.* As always, with these kinds of thoughts, Cdog dropped to the floor and started doing pushups.

***

Popeye stared at his friend and homie Gino and wondered why he couldn't just keep his mouth shut. *That drink made you weak, my boy, and I told you to leave that shit alone. You can't handle liquor. Now I gotta put your ass to sleep for all that pillow-talking you did with this loudmouth bitch. She the one that got muthafuckas looking at me sideways when I pull up in the hood.*

"Aye, you good? You don't want another cold beer?" asked Gino, who was trying to be the perfect host to Popeye, who showed up without notice at his and Linda's house.

"Maybe after we smoke some of this killa I got," Popeye said, pulling out a bag.

"That's what I'm talking about," said Gino. "I was just telling Linda you had some bomb shit in."

*And there goes the problem*, thought Popeye. *You just can't keep your mouth shut, but I got a solution for all that.* "This the last of it right here. I need to grab some more when I leave here," said Popeye.

"You need me to ride with you?" asked Gino.

*Damn*, thought Popeye, *Ima miss this nigga's loyalty to do anything with me without questioning why.* "Naw, them niggas get attitudes when you pop up with people they don't know," lied Popeye as he lit the blunt.

"Yeah, I can dig that," said Gino as he reached for the blunt. "Ima let Linda hit this." He got up and walked in the kitchen, where Linda was cooking the three of them some turkey burgers.

Popeye shook his head in thought as he sat alone in the living room. *I been knowing this nigga since third grade and gotta treat him like an enemy. I have no option in this situation. It's either run the risk of being told on and spending the rest of my life in prison or eliminate the source the info is coming from. Lord know I don't want to be lying in a cell.*

"You hear her coughing in there?" Gino asked with a big smile on his face.

"Huh?" Popeye responded, not hearing what Gino had said.

"Nigga, where your head at? You in this muthafucka straight-up daydreaming?" said Gino.

"No shit, my boy. That killa got me caught up in the moment," Popeye said. "My mouth is dry as fuck. I think I will have that beer. You and Linda enjoy the rest of that blunt."

"Yep, good looking," said Gino as he walked toward the kitchen.

Popeye watched as Gino disappeared and pulled out his gun with the silencer. He stood up and rushed into the kitchen.

Seeing him out of the corner of his eye, Gino said, "Nigga, I was gonna bring you your beer."

"I'm not gon' need it, my boy," said Popeye as he raised the gun to Linda's head, shooting her twice before her body hit the ground.

"What the fuck are—" were the last words Popeye heard his friend speak before Gino was hit in the face from a shot.

Popeye quickly moved to Gino, who was still alive. He bent over his friend, and in a soft voice with tears in his eyes, he said, "I wish it hadn't come to this. I loved you like a brother, my nigga, and if there was another option than death that would guarantee my secret, our secret, was safe, I would've took it. Trust me. This is best for you and me." Popeye shot Gino in the head once and knew that his longtime friend had gone to a better place. "Rest in peace, Gino."

Popeye stood up with tears running down his face, remembering that this was the nigga he had done damn near all his firsts with. It wasn't his brother, Hotdog, or even his cousin Tank. It was always Gino. When Popeye had gotten his first piece of pussy, it was at Gino's house. When Popeye had gone on his first mission, it was with Gino. *This was my only true friend in the world*, thought Popeye, *but this had to be done.* Anger took over the feeling of hurt, and Popeye walked over to Linda's lifeless body and shot her in the face until his gun was empty. "You made me do my boy like this, you punk bitch," he said as he walked out of the kitchen and headed for the front door.

***

"Girl, all kinds of shit been happening around here lately," said Lisa a little over a week after Gino and Linda had been found dead.

"I know. This shit got me scared to go outside right now," replied Tonya as she sat in a chair at Lisa's house, getting her hair done.

"They said Linda was shot twelve times in the face," said Nesha, shaking her head.

"These bottom niggas done did something to the wrong muthafuckas," said Tonya.

"First Big Cdog, now Gino," Nesha stated.

"Girl, and Popeye walking around the house all fucked up. He paranoid and some mo shit. I be catching his ass peeking out the window, acting like he waiting on somebody to show up," said Tonya, "and the nigga ain't touch this pussy in two weeks, so I know he tripping."

They all burst out laughing.

"Yeah, you right, girl," shot Lisa. "If your nigga ain't fuck you in two weeks and he be at home, then that nigga tripping."

"Speaking of a nigga being home, when do Tank step outta there?" asked Tonya.

"That nigga won't tell me the exact date," answered Lisa. "He think he's gon' creep up and catch me doing something. I be glad when he do come home. I was so happy when they overturned his shit."

"Well, you ain't heard it from me, but I overheard Popeye on the phone one day with Tank's momma, and he was saying to her that them niggas was in there going through some thangs, and it didn't look good for them," said Tonya.

"Naw, my Tank is straight, but that's what's wrong with the hood. Everybody in everybody business and still can't get the story right. That's why I hate muthafuckas," said Lisa.

"Bitch, don't try to get mad now that we on Tank. It was all cool a minute ago when you was all in somebody else's fucking business," said Tonya. She was starting to get a little mad at Lisa, who she had been wanting to fight anyway for a few months after hearing muthafuckas in the hood say Popeye and Lisa were fucking.

"Ain't nobody getting mad, girl. I'm just tired of all the 'he say, she say' shit around here," stated Lisa.

"Fuck all that gossip shit," said Nesha, trying to lighten the mood. "Fire up some of that killa I know Popeye done gave you to smoke since he ain't fucking you."

That made them all laugh once again and cleared the tension in the air.

"I got some too, girl," said Tonya, going into her purse.

"I'm good on smoking. Ima go lay down for a little while," said Lisa as she got up and walked to her bedroom. *Who the fuck that bitch Tonya think she is?* Lisa asked herself. *Bitch, don't speak on mine.* "But I got something for your ass," she said out loud to herself as she unhooked her cellphone from her waist and dialed a number. "Hello," Lisa said. "What you up to right now?"

"Not shit. What's good with you?" the voice on the other line asked.

"You already know," Lisa said in her sexy voice.

"Oh, you know I'm with that," the voice shot back.

"Our usual spot in thirty minutes," said Lisa.

"See you then, little momma," he said.

"And bring me some of that killa weed you got," said Lisa. "I feel like smoking."

"I got you," said Popeye as he hung up the phone.

"Yeah, bitch. He might not be fucking you, but he keep his dick in me," Lisa mumbled to herself with a smile. "I got your nigga on call."

\*\*\*

Cdog stared at his lawyer and couldn't even believe what he was saying.

"Mr. Johnson, I'm only doing my job and informing you that the DA will seek the death penalty due to you already having a life sentence and how you carried out this murder on the c/o. They are claiming you planned the whole thing." "So what are you advising me to do?" Cdog asked his lawyer, looking him in the eye.

Cooper dropped his head and whispered in a scared voice, "Take the deal they are offering you."

"*What?*" screamed Cdog, and he hit the window that separated them.

"If you don't take the deal, they are going to execute you for sure," Cooper said, now looking back up at Cdog.

"Shit, if I take the deal, I'm as good as executed," said Cdog. "That would give me two life terms, and we both know they only need one for me to die in this muthafucka."

"Mr. Johnson, it's your call on how we move forward with your case," said Cooper, "but I want you to read this." He held a paper to the window. "This is the type of evidence they got against you, so think about your options real hard for a few days, and I'll be back to see you then."

Cdog, who was still in shock from what Cooper had let him read, didn't hear anything that was just said until Cooper knocked on the window.

"You zoned out on me," said Cooper. "I know this is a lot to deal with, but you gotta decide one way or another."

All Cdog did was nod.

"I'll be back to see you," said Cooper, who turned and walked off.

Cdog sat at the window with his head down and waited to be taken back to his cell. Once back, Cdog thought of his attorney, who had been to see him three times, but this visit had Cdog both sick and steaming hot because the lawyer, against all rules, decided to share everything with him. He let Cdog read Tank's sworn statement and his promise to testify as the state eyewitness if needed.

Cdog paced his cell in thought. *That bitch-ass nigga Tank straight turned snitch and went SNY. Now I see why he wanted to do all the planning. He was setting my ass up from the start. He never wanted us to get away. The nigga just wanted it to be me and him on the yard so no one could dispute his side of the story. Now it's making sense, why he didn't want to use a weapon. The clown-ass nigga wanted everything to fall on me. My prints are the only ones on the knife,* thought Cdog. *I can't believe I didn't see the game that nigga was running.* "I was straight asleep with my eyes wide the fuck open," Cdog said. I allowed false loyalty to disarm my judgment when it came to that nigga.

"Fuck!" Cdog yelled out loud at the top of his voice. *Now just as Cooper said, I really need to weigh my options because with him being their star witness, the knife having my prints all over it and the c/o's blood all over my clothes, ain't no way I can come from under this shit. I'm gon' get the death penalty.* Cdog put his head in his hands and closed his eyes. He wanted to cry, but the tears wouldn't come out because of the different emotions he was feeling, confusing his body. His heart was pounding with pain, but his mind was screaming with anger. *How did I allow myself to love something or someone that could also drive me to wanting to destroy it or them?* He asked himself.

"Fuck the hood!" he yelled as Big Cdog being killed ran through his mind, along with the betrayal of Tank. "The hood has taken all the love I had and threw it away like some trash. You didn't teach me this part of the game, Big Cdog." He sat on his bunk, and for the next two hours, all he did was stare at the wall with a blank look on his face, not realizing or even caring that it looked like he had lost his mind.

***

Tank had paced the floor of his cell constantly for the last few days, wondering why he was still in Ad Seg. *Have they changed their mind?* He chuckled at the thought of his last question. *I can't change my mind even if I wanted to. Them niggas would have a field day with me because I'm sure the word have been sent around on what I did to Cdog.* Tank walked to his door and looked down the tier for the hundredth time that day and saw nothing moving. "This shit really is like a big-ass fucking grave," Tank said as he turned from the door. *I may as well get me a few pushups in,* he thought as he went to the floor.

After doing about forty pushups, Tank heard keys, which meant the police were doing the mail because it was too early for dinner. Tank got up from the floor and walked back to the door. He saw the c/o walking the tier coming toward his cell.

"This muthafucka ain't got no mail," Tank said to himself, looking at the empty-handed c/o.

"Aye, Adams," the c/o said as he stopped in front of Tank's door.

"What's up?" asked Tank.

"Pack all your shit up. You outta here. Don't leave nothing behind—your linen, trash, or nothing else," said the c/o. "Be ready in five."

Tank tore ass off the door and began throwing the little stuff he had onto the middle of his bunk. Once everything was on the bed, he untied the sheet from the mattress and retied the sheet around his property.

"I'm gone," said Tank really loudly with his fist in the air. *About damn time*, thought Tank as he looked around the cell for what he said would be the last time.

As promised, the c/o really was back in five minutes. "Did you get everything?" the c/o asked as he looked through the door window.

"Yeah, this muthafucka clean," answered Tank, who heard the tray slot open, and he was instructed to back up and put his hands out to be cuffed.

"Don't worry about your things. We will carry them down for you," said a c/o.

Once Tank was in cuffs, the tower was given the okay to open the door.

"Back all the way out and remain looking towards the cell," the c/o ordered.

Stepping out of the cell and onto the tier felt like fresh air had entered his lungs. Tank walked by all the muthafuckas standing at their doors, watching him. They took Tank downstairs to the c/o podium to be logged out. Tank had a perfect view of cell 121's occupant, who, just like everybody else, was standing at his door. Tank made eye contact with Cdog and smiled at him while blowing him a kiss.

Cdog was steaming hot and hollered out of his door to Tank, "You are a piece of shit, you bitch-ass nigga!"

Cdog's words had no effect on Tank, who did nothing but nod and smile even harder.

"Okay, everything checks out," said the c/o who was on the computer.

Two c/os escorted Tank toward the back door, and they had to pass cell 121.

"On Bottoms. Fuck you and your momma, nigga," replied Tank with a smile, and just like that, Tank was gone. He had officially become SNY, giving away all he had fought for growing up in the Bottoms.

"Oh, Ima kill that nigga," said Cdog as he walked from the door. He paced his cell five times before his drop to the pushup position. "Your ass is mine," he said as he went down for the first pushup.

*** Popeye had become a mess since the Gino situation. Now all he did was drink as a way to forget the pain in his heart. *I lost two brothers to this shit, and one was at my own fucking hands*, he constantly thought. The only relief he got was from the bottle or when he was sticking his dick in Lisa's mouth. Popeye realized that his at-home relationship had run its course. He hadn't touched Tonya in over a month and didn't know why because she was a pretty bitch with a stupid body.

"Yo, nigga, did you go deaf or something on me?" asked Hitman as he turned down the radio and pulled into the parking lot of the liquor store.

"Naw, dog. I just didn't hear you," answered Popeye.

"I asked what we drinking tonight?" Hitman repeated.

"Remy, of course," said Popeye as he opened the car door.

"Remy, it is," replied Hitman with a smile as he climbed from behind the wheel.

Popeye, who was already standing outside the car and took a survey of the parking lot, thought he spotted the nigga Cartoon's car. "I think we got us one," said Popeye to Hitman, who looked to where Popeye was looking.

"Is that the boy Cartoon's car?" asked Hitman, excited.

"If this is that nigga, then today just became my lucky day," said Hitman.

Cartoon was from their enemy hood and most wanted list after he had killed Boscoe a couple of months ago and then bragged about it on Facebook. Popeye pulled out his gun and crept toward the car. He looked inside, and although it was empty, he confirmed it was Cartoon's shit from the characters of Bugs Bunny, Daffy Duck, and so on all over the dashboard. Popeye walked back to Hitman and told him it was indeed Cartoon's shit.

"How you wanna do this?" asked Hitman, pulling out his gun.

"We gotta wait on the nigga out here," said Popeye. "They got too many cameras inside the store."

"Ima walk to the window and make sure it's him," said Hitman as he walked off toward the store. Just as quickly as he had left, he came jogging back. "Yep, it's him. He paying for his shit right now," said Hitman with a smile.

"Just him?" asked Popeye.

"Yep," answered Hitman.

"Ima walk to the side of the building and wait on him," said Popeye.

"Naw, he might see you and run back in the store. We got his ass, so fuck letting him get away. He don't know this car, so let's just hide behind it until he come out," suggested Hitman.

"Fo' sho'," shot Popeye.

They hid behind the car and waited with their guns out.

"Let's make sure we kill his ass this time," said Hitman. "Ain't no coming back."

Boscoe had caught Cartoon about a month before he was killed and shot him three times, but just like a cartoon character, the nigga lived and caught Boscoe slipping.

"No doubt," whispered Popeye, who found himself feeling better and not thinking of the deaths of Hotdog and Gino.

*Chirp, chirp!* They heard the car alarm.

"You go towards the front, and I'll go towards the back of the car. That way, the nigga can't run," said Popeye.

Hitman nodded. Cartoon, not paying attention to the cars in the parking lot, walked right into the ambush.

"Yo, you bitch-ass nigga. Tell the homie Boscoe we love him," said Popeye as both he and Hitman began shooting.

Cartoon never stood a chance as bullet after bullet found his body, knocking him to the ground. They both ran toward Cartoon and, without hesitation, emptied their clips. Knowing the job was done, they walked to the car and drove off.

"Yeah, nigga. That's how you treat an enemy," said Popeye as they drove back to the Bottoms.

"They gon' miss his ass over there. He was one of their main dudes. Now he RIP," said Hitman, which made Popeye look at him in a funny way.

"That nigga ain't resting in peace," said Popeye with a little anger.

"I sure hope not," said Hitman as he turned onto their block. "My RIP for him mean 'rot in piss.'"

They both burst out laughing as Hitman parked.

"'Rot in piss,'" repeated Popeye. "I like that."

***

Cdog's body had been rejecting food for the last two days. Cdog couldn't eat, shit, or sleep because of the pain in his stomach from seeing that nigga Tank. All Cdog thought of was murder. He walked back and forth in his cell, sometimes for hours, mumbling the same words: "Ima kill yo' ass." Anger had taken over his mind to the point where he wasn't thinking straight, and fighting a death penalty case never interrupted his thoughts of killing Tank. To Cdog, nothing else mattered right now.

"Johnson, I got some mail for you," said the c/o standing at the door.

Cdog walked to the door and grabbed the letters sticking in the side. He turned and walked back to his bunk, and without even looking at the envelope, he tossed the letters with four other unread ones onto his locker. He jumped up and began walking around his cell, mumbling those same four words: "Ima kill yo' ass."

Suddenly, something new happened to Cdog. Pictures of him killing Tank actually began to pop up in his head. He saw one picture where he had Tank naked and hogtied. He was melting plastic onto his body. Another picture showed him stabbing Tank over and over with a metal flat about ten inches long. He heard Tank scream in his mind, and for the first time in three days, Cdog smiled. The more he heard Tank scream, the wider his smile became. "Ima kill yo' ass," he mumbled as he got up off his bunk and continued to walk around his cell.

***

"You have a collect call from Tank," the phone said when Lisa answered. "To accept, dial or say five now."

Lisa nervously dialed five. "Hello," she said, excited.

"Hello," Tank replied, not sure it was her.

"Damn, baby. They finally let you call," said Lisa with tears in her eyes. "I missed you, Tank."

"Shit, I missed you too. I'm back on the main line now," he lied.

"I knew these sorry muthafuckas didn't know what they was talking about out here. They saying ya'll did something to a police. Then I got that nigga Junebug sending me letters, talking all kind of shit about you," said Lisa all in one breath.

"Calm down, baby. It ain't nothing like that. I got caught up in some bullshit, that's all," said Tank, "but how my baby doing?"

"Better now that I hear your voice," said Lisa. "So when can I come visit you?"

Tank thought about her question and remembered how he used to tell her to stay away from the bitches coming to this yard because whoever they were, going there to visit wasn't any good. "I can't get visits. They took my shit, and by the time I get them back, I'll be at home," he lied again to Lisa.

"That's fucked up," she said. "Have you at least been getting the letters I sent? You haven't replied to none of them."

"Naw, I ain't got one letter from your ass. Shit, I thought you left me for dead. I almost said, 'Fuck calling you,'" said Tank.

"Nigga, don't fucking play with me," said Lisa with some attitude. "I stay sending mail your way."

"When was the last time you wrote me?" asked Tank.

"I sent you a letter every time something happened in the Bottoms. So you don't know about Big Cdog?" asked Lisa.

"Naw, what about that nigga?" Tank asked back.

"They found him dead with all kind of holes in him right down the street from Karen's house," she told him. "Little Cdog ain't told you about that? I know he know."

"Get the fuck outta here. Are you serious about Big Cdog?" asked Tank.

"As a heart attack, nigga. Is that serious enough for you?" said Lisa. "But that's not all. They found Gino and his girl Linda dead in their house."

"Gino?" said Tank. "What happened?"

"Nobody know. Ain't nobody seen shit," said Lisa.

"Where is my cousin Popeye?" asked Tank.

"In the cut, like everybody else right now. That nigga Cartoon got laid out at the liquor store one night, and his homies been on one ever since," said Lisa. "Got the Bottoms looking like a ghost town. In nine months, you gon' hear about all the homies having a baby because all these niggas are laid up."

"Somebody finally caught that nigga Cartoon," Tank said just as the recording said they had two minutes remaining.

"When you gon' call again?" asked Lisa in a sad voice.

"Soon," said Tank. "Just don't let that nigga answer."

"Fuck you, nigga," Lisa said, and she laughed.

"I love you, little momma," said Tank.

"I love you more, big daddy," said Lisa.

"I'm gone," Tank said. Then he hung up the phone. He went back to his cell and lay down. This was his first official day on the yard.

*** 

Popeye, Hitman, and Cbone were sitting in Hitman's backyard, smoking weed and passing a bottle of Remy around. Hitman's red-nose pitbull was going crazy on his leash from trying to get to Popeye and Cbone.

"Kick the fuck back, Red!" yelled Hitman at his dog, who stopped for a minute and then went right back to growling.

"I don't know why his mutt ass making all that noise," said Popeye.

"If I cut him loose, your ass wouldn't be saying that shit," said Hitman.

"You right 'cause if you cut him loose, Ima pop his ass," Popeye said as he pulled out his pistol.

All three of them burst out laughing.

"But on some real shit," said Cbone, "what we gon' do about these suckas that keep coming through busting?"

Popeye and Hitman got quiet and serious when Cbone spoke. His status in the Bottoms was general.

"Haven't nobody been hit yet, but it's only a matter of time before they do," said Cbone.

"Shit, I vote we grab a few niggas and mount up. It's that nigga Cartoon's funeral today," said Hitman. The spit came flying out of his mouth right after he had said Cartoon's name, as though saying it left a bad taste.

"I'm with that," said Popeye.

Cbone looked at the young soldiers for a moment before he spoke. "Today Ima show ya'll some original shit. We don't need no one else."

Popeye and Hitman stared at their big homie. Neither one of them had actually seen Cbone put work in. They had only heard the stories from other older niggas who described Cbone as a ruthless and dangerous muthafucka. None of the young niggas had ever tested Cbone's gangsta hand because the way he pushed said he wasn't to be fucked with.

"So today is the boy's funeral, right?" asked Cbone.

"Yep," said Hitman. "Eleven o'clock on Central."

"Then it's time we show them clowns we the wrong niggas to be fucking with," Cbone said.

"Red, shut your ass up!" yelled Hitman at his dog.

"What kind of guns ya'll got?' Cbone asked.

"I got a few handguns and an AK," said Hitman.

"Handguns, AR-15, and a shotgun," Popeye added.

"Yeah, okay, but fuck them handguns. We need the big tools for this job," Cbone stated with a chuckle. "AKs and AR-15." Cbone looked at his watch, and it said ten o'clock. "We meet back here in fifteen minutes."

Cbone walked to his car, and Popeye did the same. *We about to have some fun*, thought Popeye as he drove the three blocks to his house. He ran in and grabbed his AR-15 along with three extended clips. He drove back to Hitman's house, who was in the backyard with his AK-47 and two clips that held a hundred bullets each. They heard Cbone pull up, and when he walked to the back, he was carrying his AK and a milk crate full of wine bottles. Hitman and Popeye looked at each other with confusion.

"I told ya'll we about to do some original shit to them niggas," said Cbone. "My motto is 'Don't leave a witness.' If these hot bullets don't catch their ass, then these cocktails will burn it."

"That's straight gangsta, big dog," said Popeye with a smile as he gave Cbone a fist bump.

The three of them began to stuff the gasoline-filled bottles with torn-up T-shirts Hitman had lying around in the backyard for his dog to chew on.

"This how it's gonna go down. Since they ain't on the lookout for an old nigga to come through on their ass, Ima walk right up to the church and lay down whoever in front of it. When ya'll hear this K start talking, pull the car in front of the church. Then we all rush in," said Cbone as he looked at both of them.

"Like I said before, I don't do the witness thing, so whoever standing in that church get laid down. I'm talking kids, women, the preacher, and whoever else. If ya'll ain't with that, then let me know now, and I'll take my ass back home." Cbone paused for a few seconds, and when neither one of them backed out, Cbone continued his speech. "Try to keep yourself a few bullets just in case the pigs show up because I don't know about ya'll, but me? I ain't going to jail. Now look. When I say, 'Burn,' I want ya'll to start lighting the cocktails and throw them into the church."

*Wow*, thought Popeye. *So the stories about this nigga are true. He straight up ruthless.*

"Ima ask one more time if ya'll sure this is the kind of activity ya'll ready for," said Cbone, and just like the first time he had asked that question, there was no response. Cbone smiled. "We outta here. Let's all make it back together."

They all shook hands and then headed toward the front yard.

"We can roll in this," said Cbone, pointing at a car parked at the curb.

They jumped in the car Cbone had pointed at. *And of course, this muthafucka is stolen*, thought Popeye with nothing but respect and admiration in his eyes when he looked at Cbone. *This nigga is a real one.* At eleven thirty, they pulled across the street from the church undetected. They quickly scanned their surroundings for any police that may be lurking.

"It's go time," said Cbone as he hopped out of the car with his rifle tucked and walked straight to the church.

No one was standing outside, but as soon as Cbone went through the front door, Popeye and Hitman heard shots. Popeye put the car in drive and flew to the church. When they ran in, all they could hear was screaming and gunshots. Popeye swung his AR-15 from behind his back and emptied the first clip. Hitman was doing the same with his AK-47. At almost the same time, they snatched out the empty clips and slapped in fresh ones. Bodies were falling everywhere as they couldn't escape the bullets from three high-powered rifles. "Burn this bitch down!" Cbone yelled.

They started lighting cocktails and threw them into the pews of the church. The people who had hit the floor, hiding from the bullets, jumped up when they saw the fire, and that was when Cbone went crazy with his AK-47, knocking down everything that stood up.

"We outta here!" yelled Cbone.

They all ran toward the waiting car, got in, and sped off, burning rubber in front of the church, which was now engulfed in fire. The news would later describe the scene as a ruthless, heartless, and horrific act, calling it the worst gang killing the state had ever seen in its history, where over 126 people died, and that the police had no suspects.

*** It took him four long days of pain, but Cdog fought off the hold that anger had over him. He was back to working out and ate everything they gave him for chow. He had finally gotten around to reading his mail and was heartbroken to hear how his hood was suffering with all the deaths. *First Big Cdog, now my boy Gino*, thought Cdog. *We have lost some real stand-up niggas lately, and muthafuckas out there swear they haven't seen or heard shit.* "It's all in-house. That's why," Cdog said to himself.

In one of his letters, his sister, Karen, said she couldn't do it anymore and was moving to Miami within the next couple of months. She said she had tried to convince Mom and Dad to pack up with her, but they shot the idea of moving down.

"My ass is gone though," she had said.

Cdog got off his bunk and walked to his sink, where he threw water on his face. As he was drying his face, he heard a knock on the wall. *I must be tripping*, thought Cdog. *Ain't nobody been in that cell since the Mexican moved.* But then he heard the knock again. *Somebody is over there. I been that zoned out, I didn't notice they put someone in there?* he asked himself. Then he knocked back on the wall.

"Aye, top of the day to you. I knew somebody was over there because the police put in and take out a tray every meal. I been knocking on the wall for a day and a half with no answer," the dude in cell 120 said into the vent.

"Yeah, sometime I get caught up and don't hear shit," replied Cdog. "You active?"

"Yeah, homie. I came from D-yard. I had to beat my cellie's ass," answered cell 120.

"I came from that yard too. I'm Cdog from the Bottoms," Cdog said.

"Nigga, this Curt!" shouted the dude, excited.

"What it do, my nigga?" asked Cdog with the same excitement in his voice.

"You the reason I been beating on this wall. I was trying to find out where they had you niggas," said Curt.

"I'm back here by myself. June already went to the SHU, and that bitch-ass nigga Tank went SNY," said Cdog. Then he gawked up spit and shot it in the toilet after speaking Tank's name.

"So that shit is official then?" asked Curt. "Nobody on the yard think it's true."

"Yeah, the boy went bad. I watched him walk out that back door myself a week ago. Plus, my lawyer let me read some shit on him. I'll get at you on paper about that," said Cdog.

"No doubt," said Curt. Then he asked, "So how the case looking?"

"Shit, I'm dead bang, and they talking about seeking the death penalty," answered Cdog.

"Man, that's fucked up to hear," said Curt. "Ima keep you in my prayers."

"Shit, praying ain't gon' save me," said Cdog, and he laughed. "It's ova, Curt."

"Don't talk like that, my nigga. We fight until they put us in the ground, and even then, we still move a little dirt," said Curt.

"I feel you, my boy, and I know regardless of the outcome, Ima continue to stand tall," said Cdog.

"You damn right, nigga. We built to fight this type of shit," replied Curt. "'Can't stop, won't stop, so stop asking me to.'"

They both burst out laughing at the saying all the niggas on the yard say.

"No shit," said Cdog, still laughing. "'Can't stop, won't stop, so stop asking me to.'"

"Now you sounding like my boy," said Curt.

"I can't even front, fool. You lifted my spirit," said Cdog.

"That's what friends are for," Curt started, singing in the vent, and it made both of them laugh. "I bet you ain't smoked in a while, huh?" asked Curt.

"Not since that ball you gave me," said Cdog.

"Let me get my shit right, and I got something for you," said Curt. "Keep your eye on the door for me."

"I got you," said Cdog as he stepped to the cell door.

After about twenty minutes, Curt yelled through the vent, "I'm ready! I just need to make a line."

"Don't trip. Ima put my shit right inside you cell," said Cdog.

"Nigga, you ain't been back here long enough yet to have them kind of skills," said Curt.

"Just sit back and watch me then," Cdog said as he grabbed his line and then threw it out under his door and yanked it so it would pop back toward Curt's cell.

After three attempts, Cdog heard Curt say, "Leave it right there." Curt bent down and stuck a shower shoe under his door. "I got it!" Curt yelled.

"That's them skills, my boy," said Cdog.

"Whateva," replied Curt, and he laughed. He tied an ounce of weed, some Zig-Zags, and a lighter to the line.

"Take off. It's three times," said Curt.

Cdog pulled the line, and once it was inside his cell, he confirmed getting everything by yelling, "Three times!"

"I had just over a Zip with me," said Curt. "I don't think Ima be back here after tomorrow when the captain come see me, so I'll send you the rest in the morning just in case."

"Fo' sho', my nigga," said Cdog, who was already feeling at ease. "Thank you, fool."

"It ain't nothing to a real nigga for a real nigga," said Curt, and he started singing "That's What Friends Are For" again, and again, they burst out laughing.

"Let me get my head right," said Cdog.

"On the real," replied Curt.

Afterward, Cdog and Curt spent half the night on the vent, with Curt catching Cdog up on all the latest shit going down on the yard and on the streets. The next day, as predicted, Curt was sent back to D-yard.

"Stay safe, my boy!" yelled Cdog out of the door as Curt was being escorted out the back.

"You too! Love and respect!" shouted Curt.

"No doubt," replied Cdog as he watched his boy disappear.

***

Tank realized fast that the SNY yard had about the same, if not more, politics than the main line. He noticed that you could sit at any table with any race, you could be in a cell with whomever you chose, and you could play any table game or sport with any race, unlike on the general population main line, where you were restricted to your own race, period. The political line being pushed on the SNY yard was the direct opposite of everything Tank stood and fought for on the main line. Here, he found out that your status was based on how many people you had told on. Child molesters ran together, and just like on the main line, they were looked down on, but no one did anything to them here.

The group of inmates who, without a doubt, ran the SNY yard, Tank noticed, were the homosexuals. They were everywhere, and they were being followed by some niggas who, at one time, were considered stand-up until the dropout. Tank knew in his heart that these weren't the people he should be around, which made him antisocial. One day, after Tank got out of the shower and went downstairs to the TV area, a dude approached him, and Tank knew immediately the dude was gay.

"Hi, my name is Porsche," the dude said, smacking his lips.

Tank looked at him with disgust and, in calm voice, replied, "You can take your show somewhere else 'cause I don't swang."

"Damn. Like that?" asked Porsche, raising his eyebrows.

"Just like that, nigga," Tank said with a lot of aggression.

"I just wanted to introduce myself, that's all, and let you know I'm the program clerk if you ever need anything, Tank," said Porsche.

The look on Tank's face changed from anger to "How the fuck this fag know my name?"

Porsche, reading Tank's face all the way, quickly stated, "Like I told you, I'm the program clerk. I type up damn near every sheet of paper that has to do with this yard. I knew you was coming before you did, sweetheart."

"Since you know my name, then don't ever call me sweetheart again," said Tank, now looking Porsche in the eye, "and there's nothing at all you can do for me."

Porsche smacked his lips and gave Tank two snaps in the air and then turned and walked off, swishing his ass. From that day forward, Tank didn't have another encounter like that with another homosexual. Porsche, who ran the gays on the entire yard, put the word out to stay clear of Tank.

ll Tank did was work out and mind his own business. Some nights, the soul of the real nigga he used to be would visit him while he lay on his bunk and try to encourage him to get back to who he was—the nigga who had loyalty and the upmost respect for the game, the nigga who had once made it his job to keep these people he was now surrounded by on the run. Tank fought with this spirit with all the strength inside of him. "I can't go back," he would say out loud. "I did some shit ain't no coming back from."

\*\*\* Popeye and Hitman were laid back in Popeye's car, smoking a blunt and shooting the shit.

"Nigga, I think I would have rather had them bustas coming through with their little popping than these muthafucking police," said Hitman.

"No shit. I feel you on that. They been kicking in doors to spots I didn't even know the homies had," said Popeye, laughing.

"I know. Huh, I seen them kick in the Mexican bitch's door the other day and pulled that nigga Blue up outta there. The Mexican bitch don't even speak English, nigga," said Hitman, "and I know Blue's dumb ass can't speak Spanish."

They both laughed until tears ran down their faces. Ever since Hitman had become his everyday nigga, Popeye thought about the past less often. He still missed Hotdog and Gino, but the shit he and Hitman had been on lately eased his pain because he had less time to dwell on it.

"Blue a fool for that," said Popeye. "I wonder how they talk to each other."

"With hand signs, nigga," said Hitman, and they started laughing again. "But trip, on a serious note, we put some major work in for the hood"— Hitman paused to let his words sink in before he continued—"but I ain't never fucking with Cbone on that level again."

"Yeah, that nigga proved to me he deserve to be the general," replied Popeye, "and if any of these young niggas get out of line with him, Ima lay their ass down. He ain't even gonna have to ask."

"Shit, that's if he don't beat you to the punch," said Hitman, which sent them back to uncontrollable laughter.

"Fucking with him made shit hit the news. Muthafuckas all over the state know that was us but can't prove it. Got everybody scared shitless. They know the Bottom niggas are the wrong niggas to fuck with," said Popeye as he smiled proudly.

"Yep, on the real. That shit got both niggas and bitches talking about it," replied Hitman.

"That's because our generation ain't seen no shit like that. We so used to seeing drive-bys where sometime nobody get shot. You can best believe the police know an OG nigga called that," said Popeye.

"The only thing left to do now is start taking over their turf," shot Hitman.

"My nigga, quiet as it kept, I think Cbone already doing that. I drove down the main block they used to be on, and it was a ghost town, but I see Cbone come out a house and sit on the porch with a beer," said Popeye.

"No shit?" asked Hitman. "I told you that nigga crazy."

"I blew the horn at him and kept pushing," said Popeye. "Talking about beer now, I feel like drinking."

"I can do that," said Hitman as Popeye started the car, and they drove off, headed to the liquor store.

***

Junebug was curled up on his bunk, feeling straight-up sick inside. He had felt that way since receiving the letter from his little brother telling him how shit had been in the Bottoms the last few months, but what had Junebug sick was what his brother had said about Lisa.

"She look like shit, big bro. You need to stop asking about her and focus more on your daughter, who, by the way, be with Nesha more than anybody. Lisa is in her own lane, bro, and it's only a matter of time before she run off the road."

Junebug kept hearing these words in his head until they actually made him sick. *She just need me*, he thought. *My love for her can make her bounce back from whatever she going through.* Junebug was straight-up living in an illusion, where reality meant nothing. All he saw was him and Lisa being happy and with each other. In his twisted mind, Junebug saw no wrong that Lisa could do. It was just niggas like Tank who took advantage of her, and his little brother didn't know what the fuck he was talking about. *My baby still look good*, he thought as he glanced up to the top bunk at the picture of Lisa. *She one of the baddest females in the Bottoms, and any nigga would be on her.*

Suddenly, like a light being turned on, Junebug's mind told him that was the problem. His brother wanted Lisa. "That nigga trying to get me to leave her so he can holla," Junebug said. "It ain't gon' happen, nigga, because she mine." Starting to feel better after discovering why his brother had said those things about Lisa made Junebug grab his pen and paper and write his little brother a three-page letter telling him how full of shit he was to say those things about Lisa, knowing they weren't true. "And from this day forward, you are dead to me." Junebug ended the letter by saying in all capital letters for him to "*STAY AWAY FROM LISA.*"

\*\*\*

Tank got up off his bunk and walked to his cell door. He hit his light switch up and down a few times to get the tower's attention.

"What can I do for you, cell 239?" asked the tower cop over the mic.

"I got a phone call!" yelled Tank out the side of his door.

The c/o glanced at his watch and then took a look at the phone list. Seeing Tank's name, he opened the cell door.

"You are on phone two," the tower said to Tank, who was walking down the stairs and gave the c/o a thumbs-up.

Tank walked across the dayroom to phone two and told the dude on it that it was his time. After about thirty seconds and a quick wipe-down of the phone, Tank was dialing Lisa's number. He said his name after the beep, and the phone rang.

After three rings, Lisa answered and heard the recording say that she had a collect call from Tank. She immediately hit the five button on her phone. "Hey, baby," she said in her sexy voice, even though she felt like shit.

"It sure took forever for you to accept my call," Tank said, playing. "Hey, back at you anyway."

"No, nigga, it didn't take a long time for me to answer. The phone only rung twice, but what did take a long time was you calling me back. You must've called your other bitch," said Lisa.

"Yeah, I did, but she was on some bullshit when I called," shot back Tank, but quickly, he added, "You know damn well ain't no other bitch."

"Let me find out, Tank," said Lisa, "but I'm glad you called though. I seen your cousin, and he asked if you was good."

"Who? Popeye?" asked Tank.

"Naw, nigga, the pope. Yeah, Popeye," answered Lisa, and they both laughed.

"Hell naw. I ain't good. I need some money for canteen," said Tank. "Call the nigga on three-way."

Lisa's heart began to beat quickly. She knew once Popeye saw it was her number calling his phone, he would answer with some slick shit, thinking she was hitting him for a booty call. *Think, Lisa*, she told herself, but it was as if her mind wouldn't click.

"Did you hear me?" asked Tank.

"Yeah, baby. I'm looking for his number," she lied. *Where the fuck is Nesha when I need her?* Lisa asked herself. She put the phone on speaker so she could still talk with Tank while she sent Popeye a text, letting him know she was about to call him with Tank on the phone. "So don't say no crazy shit when you answer." She pushed the "Send Text" button and then said to Tank, "Oh, here's his number right here."

Popeye texted back, "Okay," as she was telling Tank that last lie.

"Hold on, baby," said Lisa, and she clicked the line to do the three-way. She clicked back over when she heard Popeye's ringback playing. It was "Bid Long" by Plies.

"What up?" said Popeye.

"That song, my nigga," replied Tank.

"Yeah, he saying some real shit on that song, but what's good, cuzzo?" asked Popeye.

"One day closer to the house," answered Tank.

"They out here talking about some wild shit that ya'll got going on in there with the police. So when are you coming, nigga? And I don't want to hear that 'soon' shit. I need you out here," said Popeye.

"He ain't gon' tell you while I'm on the phone," said Lisa.

"I don't blame him," shot Popeye, which made Tank laugh, but Popeye was thinking about how he had Lisa's ass in the air just last night.

"Fuck both of ya'll," said Lisa.

"Get off my girl, nigga," said Tank "I'll be there soon."

"And there you go with that 'soon' shit. I know you hearing about all this wild shit going on out here," said Popeye.

"Yeah, I caught a word or two. I need you to be careful until I get there, my boy. Auntie can't take another loss. She might have a nervous breakdown," said Tank.

"Man, I'm good. These niggas don't wanna see me," said Popeye, getting hyped. "You ain't setting the right word if you ain't heard that I run this shit."

Tank, seeing where the conversation was headed with the police, more than likely listening, changed the subject before Popeye said something he would later regret. "I need a few dollars for store," said Tank.

"You know I got you when you need it?" asked Popeye.

"Shit, ASAP," answered Tank.

"I'll have it on your account today. You know I'm not putting shit in Lisa's hands," said Popeye, and they both laughed again.

"Oh, so that shit funny, Tank?" Lisa asked in a serious tone.

"Naw, baby, calm down. He ain't doing nothing but playing with your ass," said Tank.

"Shit if I am," said Popeye, "but Ima hook you up today, and from now on, you can hit my line direct. Fuck this three-way shit. I got money on my phone for collect calls."

"Okay, I will, cuzzo. I love you," said Tank.

"I love you too, foo'. Fuck you, Lisa," said Popeye, laughing as he hung up.

"I can't stand his ugly ass. I'm not ever calling him for you again," said Lisa, playing like she was mad, but she couldn't wait to call Popeye back later tonight.

"Man, knock that shit off. You know damn well he don't mean that," said Tank, who was starting to get mad at Lisa.

She sensed Tank's anger and said in a soft voice, "Okay, big daddy. I know you wouldn't let no one disrespect me."

The recording cut in before Tank could respond to her last comment. "Ima call you back first chance I get, but hit Popeye later and make sure he did that for me," said Tank.

"I will. I love you, big daddy," said Lisa.

"I love you too. I'm gone," said Tank, and he hung up the phone.

***

Cdog was becoming frustrated. They were slowly killing him with dry runs to court. It started to be that every time he went, either his lawyer was away on another appearance and his fill-in had no clue of his case or the DA was a no-show. Cdog had made up his mind that enough was enough. There was no reason to prolong the inevitable. *I'm gonna be found guilty.* That's where Cdog's frame of mind was when Cooper had come to the holding tank to talk to him.

"Look, man," said Cdog, "I've been shackled and dragged down here four times this month and haven't seen the judge."

Cooper had just told him that the DA was away on another case and that they wouldn't be seeing the judge again today. "I know," shot Cooper, "but cases like yours take time. The judges don't fool around on death penalty cases. They make sure everything is done by the book."

"I understand all that, but what about my rights to a speedy trial?" asked Cdog.

Cooper looked at Cdog with a serious look before he spoke, making sure they both understood each other because in Cooper's mind, it sounded like a new angle he could use to attack the case. "Only a crazy person would rush a death penalty case. You ain't crazy, are you?" Cooper asked.

"Why would you ask me something like that?" shot Cdog with his own question.

"Because insanity, for sure, keeps you off death row," answered Cooper.

"Naw, man. I'm not crazy. I'm just tired of the runaround game," said Cdog.

"Have you ever heard the term 'Do it until they can take no more'?" asked Cooper, and he raised his eyebrows.

"So they trying to wear me down," said Cdog.

"You ain't heard that from me," shot Cooper

"So when do I come back and actually see the judge?" asked Cdog.

"They gave us a court date for two weeks from today, but there's no guarantee we will be in front of the judge then. You have to kick back and let this case run its course," said Cooper.

"Man, fuck this case and its course. I'm tired of the back-and-forth shit. I'm ready for this shit to be over with no matter what the outcome is," said Cdog.

Cooper, at first, didn't say anything. He just stared at Cdog, knowing that he was close to taking the deal, which, to Cooper, meant he had done his job of keeping this young black dude off death row. From the beginning, this was an open-and-shut case for the DA. Cdog was caught red-handed. Plus, the other guy turned state against him, but the DA owed Cooper one big time, and Cooper decided that Cdog's case, after only meeting him once, would be the one to collect his debt from the DA. There was something different in this young dude, Cooper had thought. He just didn't look like someone who should be sitting up on death row, waiting to die.

"We will get this done, Mr. Johnson. Just give me a little time to get the wheels moving. Trust me. I'm on your side with this," said Cooper, being sincere.

Cdog could feel the honesty coming from the man he barely knew. "Okay, Coop. It's in your hands. Ima trust you until you prove otherwise," Cdog said.

"I will try to not let you down," replied Cooper as he stood up. "Two weeks, we are back here."

"Yep," said Cdog as the police opened the door to let Cooper out.

\*\*\*

"Popeye, what you want for dinner?" asked Tonya, standing at the front door of their house, on her way to the store.

"I ain't tripping. Whateva you make, Ima knock it down," said Popeye, who lately had been doing all the things that made Tonya fall in love with him all over again.

"Okay, so when I drag some octopus through this door, I don't wanna hear your mouth say nothing," she said. "Hitman, you staying for dinner?"

"Not if you cooking that shit," answered Hitman, and all three of them laughed.

"I feel like pork chops," said Tonya.

"That's cool," Popeye replied.

"Then I'm staying if it's pork chops," shot Hitman.

Tonya shook her head at them and walked out the door.

"Now that baby is gone, let's finish discussing that business," said Hitman.

"Okay, trip. Like I said earlier, I low-key been peeping this spot out the Mexicans got," said Popeye. "Nigga, it's more traffic at that muthafucka than a grocery store."

"What they doing?" asked Hitman.

"I'm not sure, but I stay seeing fools walk in with bags, and they be jumping outta some hot whips. They doing something big in there," answered Popeye.

"If they keep traffic like you said, then how we supposed to get in?" Hitman asked.

"Since I been watching, they shut everything down at the same time every day. Nobody goes in, and nobody comes out," said Popeye.

"So how the fuck we supposed to get in?" asked Hitman once again.

"We break in, my nigga," answered Popeye. "I got all the tools we need."

"Burglary ain't really ever been my thang," said Hitman, "but I know a few niggas that flock, and they stupid up right now."

"I'm telling you, it's in there, and it got our names on it. Nigga, we just gotta go get it," replied Popeye, trying to convince Hitman, who, after a few seconds of thinking, made up his mind.

"Fuck it. When do we go?" asked Hitman.

"Shit, we can do it tomorrow night," said Popeye, who then spent the next hour laying out how they would do it. He ended by saying, "It's that simple, my boy."

"Tomorrow night it is then," said Hitman.

They spent the rest of their night drinking and smoking and ended with the bomb-ass pork chops Tonya had made.

"So I'll see you tomorrow," said Hitman, walking out the front door.

"Yep," replied Popeye. "Bottoms, nigga."

"Bottoms," repeated Hitman.

The next night found them standing in the backyard of the Mexicans' house. They both had on all black to blend in with the night. Standing at the back door, Popeye put his ear against the window and listened for about five minutes for any sound coming from inside the house. Satisfied that it was clear, he pulled out the window cutter and began cutting the glass in a circle, big enough to stick his hand through. He placed the suction cup onto the circle of the cut glass and pulled. Popeye looked through the hole into the house, and after seeing nothing, he stuck his hand in and unlocked the door. He pushed it open inch by inch, trying to make no noise. When the door was halfway open, they crept inside the house with guns out and ready to shoot. They looked around the entire first floor of the house before feeling comfortable enough to go upstairs. There were three bedrooms and one bathroom on the second floor of the house.

Popeye pointed to two doors and then pointed to Hitman, signaling those were his to clear. As he walked toward one of the other doors, Popeye slowly turned the knob and pushed the door open. It was empty—no bed, no dresser, no nothing. He walked to the closet, and just like the room, it too was empty. Hitman walked to the door of one of his rooms and found it in the exact same shape as Popeye had found his—empty. Backing out into the hallway, they both stood in front of the remaining room. Popeye pointed at Hitman and then to himself as he turned the knob and began pushing the door open. This room was fully furnished, and as Popeye's eyes fell on the bed, he saw two bodies lying in it. He held up the number two at Hitman. They moved into the room swiftly, with one of them on each side of the bed. They pointed their weapons at the two who were asleep.

"Wake your ass up," said Popeye as he swung his gun down onto the man's head, causing a big gash.

"Hey, what the fuck you do?" asked the Mexican man, trying to sit up.

Popeye hit him again with the gun. "If you make another move, Ima blow your fucking face off," said Popeye.

The woman was awake and just lay there with her eyes wide open.

"Turn on that lamp," said Popeye to Hitman.

When the light came on, they couldn't believe who they saw lying on the bed. They were two old-ass Mexicans. The lady looked to be around seventy and the man even older.

"We only came here for the money, so don't make us take your life with us as well," said Popeye. "Where is the money?"

"Me no English," said the Mexican man as he looked up at them.

Popeye hit him across the head. "You know English, muthafucka. You spoke it real good when I woke your ass up," Popeye said, and then he hit him again.

"Me no English, my friend," said the man in pain.

Popeye hit him again and again before the lady finally spoke.

"It in the fucking closet!" she shouted.

"Gloria, shut your mouth," ordered the man.

"Just take the money and leave," she said.

Popeye nodded toward the closet, and Hitman walked to it. He open the door and saw a big-ass duffel bag on the floor, so he bent down and unzipped it. He saw nothing but bundles of cash inside, which made him shake at first because he had never seen that much money at one time.

"Jackpot," said Hitman with a smile.

"Both of ya'll, get up now," demanded Popeye.

"You got the money, so just leave us be. We won't call the police," said the man.

"I told you to get your ass up," Popeye said again and then struck the man.

That last blow made both of them move. They were taken downstairs and ordered to sit in chairs. Popeye yanked out the phone cord from the wall and used it as a rope to tie them up.

"Now I'm only gonna ask this one time. Is there any more money in here?" asked Popeye, standing in front of the couple.

"You got everything," said the man.

"Oh, so you speak English now, huh?" said Popeye, and he noticed that the lady kept looking toward a door with a big-ass padlock on it. "What's in there?" Popeye asked.

"Nothing," answered the lady really quickly.

"Then why is there a lock on the door?" asked Popeye, but neither the lady nor the man said anything. "Okay, I'm about to find out what nothing is and why it gotta be under lock and key." Popeye reached into his backpack for the lock cutter.

"No," said the woman. "Please just leave."

Popeye ignored her and walked to the door. He snapped the lock and opened the door. The shit that hit his nose smelled like straight death. "What the fuck ya'll got down there? Some dead bodies?" Popeye asked as he hit the light switch.

He looked down the stairs, and what he saw scared the shit out of him. Looking back up at him were the numerous eyes of Mexicans—kids, women, and men. They were dirty and looked like most had been beaten. They had three bodies lying at the bottom of the stairs, which explained the smell.

"What the fuck?" Popeye was finally able to say. Then it hit him. *This is one of those human traffic rings.* "We gotta go," he said to Hitman.

"What's down there, nigga?" asked Hitman as he walked to the door. "Damn" was all he could say as he looked down at the Mexicans.

Popeye walked back to the couple tied up and looked at them while shaking his head. "I guess we will be leaving with ya'll life after all," he said as he put a bullet into each of their heads.

He and Hitman grabbed the duffel bag and backpack and then started for the door.

Popeye stopped and turned back to the basement door. "Y'all can leave when we do," said Popeye, but the Mexicans had blank stares on their faces. So he yelled the little Spanish he knew to them—"Adelante!" which meant, "Go ahead."

\*\*\* Junebug walked the floor of his cell, and for some unknown reason, he felt better today than he had for a while. He did himself a Jane Fonda workout, which was something he hadn't done in months. Even Lisa wasn't the focus of his attention today. He sat on his bunk and read a few pages from a book he had been reading off and on for two months. He heard the keys jingling, which meant the c/o was passing out mail. Junebug didn't even move. Usually, he would stand at the door, wishing and praying there was a letter for him, but today was different, which even made the c/o stop at his door.

"Robinson, you all right today?" asked the c/o.

"Yeah, I'm good, man," answered Junebug, sitting on his bunk with his book.

The c/o looked at him for a few seconds and then moved on down the tier. Junebug closed his book and grabbed his cup to make some coffee.

"Ima write me a poem to my muthafuckin' self," he said while standing at his sink, waiting for the water to get hot.

Poems were something Junebug was good at. He just stopped writing them because of the many distractions in his head, but once again, today he felt different. He grabbed for his pen and paper and sat at the desk in his cell, and for a moment, he just thought. Then he began to write.

### ~~~ *I'm In Too Deep* ~~~

*I lie down, but from the nightmares, I just can't sleep; I'm in too deep*
*Walking this cell is like being stuck in quicksand*
*The more I move, the more I feel weak; I'm in too deep*
*The board denied me parole for five more years; I'm in too deep*
*On the yard, I wear shades to hide the tracks of my tears; I'm in too deep*
*I lie in my bed, and my mind won't leave the past; I'm in too deep*
*While fighting my case, my girl said she would have my back forever*
*But damn, forever came fast; I'm in too deep*
*Family and friends by my side, I can count on one hand; I'm in too deep*
*They say the heart won't forgive what the mind can't forget; I'm in too deep*
*I think my momma going crazy 'cause in her letter, she*
*swear this all part of God's plan; I'm in too deep*
*They say the heart won't forgive what the mind can't forget; I'm in too deep*
*Then forgiveness is a long way from me 'cause my mind keep saying, "Not yet"*
*I'm in too deep, I'm in too deep*

"I like that," said Junebug as he stood up from the desk. "I'm in too fucking deep." Then he dropped the pen as though it were a mic.

\*\*\*

"Girl, did you see the news?" asked Lisa.

"Naw, why?" Nesha answered as they sat in their living room.

"Not too far from here, they found two people tied up and killed," said Lisa. "Some old-ass people too, but the cold part is what the police found in their basement."

"What they find?" asked Nesha, who was now interested in the conversation.

"They found four more bodies that they think died from starvation. The news also said that the police believe the house was being used as a storage spot for a human traffic operation," said Lisa, shaking her head.

"Damn, in our neighborhood," said Nesha. "Were they black?"

"Bitch, you know damn well ain't no niggas involved in shit like that. It was them fucking Mexicans," answered Lisa.

"Them muthafuckas stay doing something stupid," said Nesha. Then she changed the subject by asking, "Did you go to the doctor yet?"

"Hello? I could've sworn my momma was dead," said Lisa with an attitude.

"You know what? I'm tired of your shit, Lisa. If it's going to take me kicking your ass for you to get yourself together, then I will do it," said Nesha, now in her sister's face.

Although Nesha was her little sister of three years, Lisa knew she couldn't fuck with Nesha from the shoulders. The bitch had hands when it came to fighting, but Lisa was a real Bottoms bitch who wasn't scared and accepted her sister's challenge. "Bitch, you ain't gon' do shit to me," said Lisa in a loud voice.

That was all Nesha needed to hear. She slapped Lisa so hard, it knocked her to the floor. "Naw, bitch, get your ass up. We about to do this," said Nesha, snatching out her earrings. "I been waiting to whip your ass."

Lisa got back up to her feet and rushed at Nesha, swinging with her head down. Nesha took two quick steps backward and then, with all her strength, hit Lisa with an uppercut, which made Lisa raise her head. That was when Nesha hit her with a right cross and then a hard left jab to the nose that started gushing blood on impact, but Nesha wasn't done with her. Seeing that her big sister was no match to her with bald fists, Nesha began slapping her with both hands. When it looked like Lisa was about to fall one way, Nesha slapped her back the other way.

"You dumb, tramp-ass bitch! Get your life together!" Nesha screamed while slapping her.

Lisa tried to run, but Nesha grabbed her shirt with one hand and continued to slap her with the other hand.

"I been watching every fucking thing you been doing, bitch!" *Slap!* "This is what you wanted, huh?" *Slap!* Nesha slapped her so many times, her palm became numb, and that was when she let her sister go.

Lisa fell to the floor with a bloody face and screamed, "I'm sorry!" over and over.

"You need to tell your daughter that!" Nesha screamed back. "I'm not dealing with your ass anymore from here on out." Nesha walked to her bedroom and grabbed a few of her things. She walked back to the living room, and Lisa was still lying on the floor. "I'll be back for the rest of my shit soon," said Nesha.

"Please don't leave, Nesha. I need you. Ima get myself together," said Lisa, crying.

"I'm out this muthafucka," said Nesha, and she slammed the door when she left.

"Nesha! Nesha!" screamed Lisa, but Nesha was already in her car, pulling off.

***

Cdog sat in his cell and thought of his next move. *Do I say 'Fuck it' and go to trial and see if this nigga can look me in the eye and still testify against me? Or shit, what if I go proper and represent myself? Would I be allowed to approach the witness stand? Naw, they wouldn't allow me to get that close to that rat-ass nigga. I think Cooper may be right. This one of those times where you gotta tap out and live to fight another day. I know that you can't play with these muthafuckas if your money ain't long and that the court system has fucked over countless niggas like me who couldn't afford the right lawyer. A punk-ass two-dollar ink pen has taken more lives than the average gun on the street. All the judge gotta do is sign his name with that ink pen, and a nigga's life is over,* thought Cdog. *I really only have one option if I plan to keep breathing because after about ten years of appealing the death sentence, which would just be a stall tactic on my part, I'll be executed, but if I take the deal, there's a chance. Although in prison, I could live to be an old man. Plus, I got some unfinished business to take care of.*

Cdog got up from his bunk and walked around his cell floor. Out loud to himself, he began to curse everyone who had a connection to Tank living. "Fuck his momma for having him. Fuck his daddy for the wasted sperm." He even went on to curse the doctor and the nurse who had help delivered Tank. *I can't let this nigga win,* thought Cdog, *but then again, I may not have a choice.* "The police already did count, so it's smoke time," he said, and he smiled. "Thank god for my boy Curt."

***

Tank hated everything about his job in the kitchen, but he especially hated when he saw how muthafuckas used the inmate bathrooms as a hotel. He watched as nigga after nigga snuck in there with homosexuals, doing what they did, and then came back out and worked on the food tray line. Between that and the Mexicans sneaking in to shoot their dope, the bathrooms were being used for everything except bathroom business.

One day Tank had reached his boiling point and confronted one of the black dudes who had gone in and out of the restroom all the time with one of the homosexuals.

"Ayee, homie," said Tank. "You are one of the cooks that gotta touch and stand over our food, so why do you keep running your ass in there with that fag?"

"For one thing, brah, my business is my business. Second, don't call my girl the F-word again," said the dude.

"Nigga, if you got your grimy ass over what I'm about to eat, then that is my business, and for the record, that ain't no girl. That's a fucking man, so that makes you a fag also," said Tank.

"We gotta get down, brah, for all that disrespecting you doing," the dude said, and he walked toward the restroom. He opened up the door and went inside, waiting on Tank to follow.

Tank smiled because this was exactly what he was looking for when he had confronted the dude.

"Come on in and close the door, brah," the dude said with confidence.

*Oh, I'm about to beat this nigga's ass*, thought Tank as he walked in and closed the door.

"So what was that shit you was talking out there, brah?" the dude asked.

Tank didn't even answer him with words. He instead did two hard punches that broke the dude's jaw and knocked him out. "Fucking fag," said Tank to the guy, who was on the floor, out cold.

Tank walked out of the bathroom and saw the homosexual run in. Just knowing without a doubt he would get a write-up for the fight, Tank said, "Fuck work" and went back to his cell, where he waited on the police to come get him. All night, he waited, but no police came to his door. Instead, early the next morning, Porsche came to his cell.

"Aye, Tank, top of the morning. I just came by to let you know you don't have to worry about a write-up or anything else from what happened last night. I took care of that. I'm glad somebody finally beat his ass. He always hitting on his girlfriend. Ima get you unassigned from the kitchen too," said

Porsche as Tank stood at the door, quiet. "Dang. A bitch can't get a thank-you or nothing?" asked Porsche.

"How about you get the fuck away from my door?" said Tank.

"Still the same old nigga, I see. Okay, that's cool. You welcome," said Porsche, and he walked off.

Tank felt relieved that he wouldn't be written up and happy to be leaving the kitchen. He sat on his bunk and smiled, knowing he had gotten away with an assault, which would've added six months to his time or sent him back to the hole. "I gotta kick my ass back," said Tank as he thought about how close he was to going home. "I'm almost there."

\*\*\*

"What's the deal, my boy?" asked Popeye when Hitman opened the door.

"Just laid back," answered Hitman, who was still in his PJs.

"I can see that," said Popeye as he looked Hitman up and down and then laughed.

They hadn't hung out together since the night of the burglary.

"That was some nice little change," said Popeye, referring to the money they took.

"Hell yeah, close to 150 racks each," said Hitman with a smile.

"Them old-ass Mexicans was straight slanging people. Fuck some dope," Popeye replied. "That's the type of shit going on in the hood, and we had no clue. Them muthafuckas was making all that money and moving bodies in and out, and nobody from the Bottoms knew shit."

"I know, nigga. Make me want to start running up in all these Mexicans' houses," said Hitman.

"On the real," Popeye replied, "and them muthafuckas be having fat shit parked in their driveways and want us to think it's from selling oranges and flowers on the freeway off ramp."

They both laughed at that.

"Them fools be connected to all kind of shit. They need to turn niggas on their game since them living and doing the shit in our hood," said Hitman in a serious voice.

"They ain't gon' do that," said Popeye. "They know already that niggas take over shit when they get in, so them Mexicans gon' keep shit like that among themselves."

"Yeah, you right about that," said Hitman. "So what you got planned with your money?" he asked.

"Shit, honestly, I haven't thought about that. I'm just going with the flow and having a little fun. I'm happy being hood rich right now," said Popeye. "What about you?"

"Me, myself, I'm looking for something legal I can get into. A nigga can't live his life like this forever. I love the hood until death, but that don't mean I want the hood to be the reason for my death," said Hitman.

"Look at you, trying to sound all smart and shit," said Popeye, and he laughed.

"I'm serious, my nigga. Me and you have put in some major work for the hood. I say since we got us a few dollars, it's time we start playing the background and let some of these other niggas put their life on the line," Hitman said.

Popeye thought about what his boy was saying, and he felt every word of it. He knew in his heart that they couldn't keep shooting up the town and getting away with it. "You saying some real shit, but at the same time, we both know it ain't that easy to just walk away from this life," said Popeye.

"I'm not saying let's just up and walk away. I'm saying it's time we become smarter with our moves," said Hitman. "Just like a baby who learn to crawl before they walk, we need to start crawling away until it's time to walk away." Hitman paused and then added, "I don't want to be just carried away from this muthafucka like most niggas who didn't realize their time in the hood was overdue."

All Popeye could do was listen to the wisdom Hitman was sharing with him. "It's a lot to think about," said Popeye, "so give me some time."

"Fo' sho'," Hitman said. "Now let me get dressed so we can hit the block."

"Now there go the nigga I'm talking about," said Popeye, and he laughed. Popeye never got the chance to let Hitman know that he had decided to follow his advice and start playing the background. He had become tired of the monster he had grown into. Plus, he wanted to give Tonya the life she deserved. He had fallen in love with her all over again. She had put up with all his bullshit and still remained by his side.

Three days after the talk with Hitman, they sat in Popeye's car, smoking a blunt. Popeye was in thought about how to tell his comrade of his desire for change when flashing lights appeared behind them, catching them both off guard.

"What the fuck?" asked Hitman as he took a look back.

"Damn," said Popeye. "Tuesday and Thursday." These were the days the gang unit ran around the hoods like they heard that Osama bin Laden was kicking it with the homies.

"It's that bitch-ass nigga Ross," Popeye said.

"Fuck," said Hitman.

Ross was the lead gang officer for that area, and he was known for planting shit on muthafuckas.

"It's three of 'em. One just jumped out the back seat," said Popeye as he looked in his rearview mirror.

"Why they fucking with us?" asked Hitman to himself, but Popeye thought he was asking him that question.

"Shit, I don't know, but we about to find out," answered Popeye.

He watched one of the officers go to Hitman's side of the car, and Ross came to the driver side. All three officers had their guns out.

"Popeye, I need you to reach slowly and pull the keys out the ignition and toss them out the window!" yelled Ross, standing at the back driver side of Popeye's car with his gun aimed at the driver-side window.

Popeye took the keys from the ignition and threw them to the street, not even thinking about why they had their guns out because every traffic stop in the hood began with the police having their guns down your throat.

"Damn, Ross, why ya'll rolling up on us like this? We was parked and wasn't doing shit!" yelled Popeye.

"Just hold on. We will sort it all out in a few minutes," answered Ross as he said a code into his radio.

Seconds later, four black-and-white patrol cars magically appeared.

"This ain't no traffic stop," said Hitman.

"I know, and they got the drop on us," replied Popeye, looking around. Then out of nowhere, the shit they had done at that church popped into his mind. "I knew we shouldn't have fucked with Cbone on that shit," said Popeye.

"You think that's what this is about?" asked Hitman.

"Look how they acting, nigga. They scared to come to the car," answered Popeye.

"Popeye, I need you to step out the car with your hands in the air and face away from me!" yelled Ross.

Popeye climbed out of the car and did as told.

"Go to your knees and keep your hands up," said Ross. "Passenger, you stay in the car with your hands up."

A crowd had started to gather, and Popeye heard someone shouting, "They ain't did shit! You always fucking with somebody, Ross, with your bitch ass!"

"Popeye, go to your stomach and put your arms straight ahead with your hands palm side up," said Ross.

Popeye was now lying in the middle of the street, looking like he was flying.

"Passenger, it's your turn. Get out and do the same routine," demanded another officer.

Hitman got out of the car with his hands up and went to his knees and then lay on the sidewalk. He too looked as though he were flying.

"Don't move!" yelled Ross as he and two more officers snuck up on the car, pointing their weapons toward it. Finding no one inside, Ross gave the all-clear signal, and officers swarmed Popeye and Hitman at the same time, snatching their arms so hard and fast, they almost broke.

"Y'all ain't gotta be doing all that! They already on the ground!" some yelled from the crowd.

After being cuffed, both of them were stood up and searched again, even though they had just searched on the ground.

"Popeye, I been looking for you," said Ross. Then he glanced at Hitman. Ross's face lit up as he said, "Is that you, Hitman? I been looking for you too."

I ain't did shit, so you looking for me," asked Popeye.

"We will talk at the station, but let me just say all that playing peek-a-boo behind a car in a liquor store parking lot ain't cool at all, Popeye," said Ross, and he laughed. "Put them in separate cars, and get 'em the fuck outta here before we have a riot to deal with," he ordered to the officers while looking at the police station.

Popeye was sitting in the interrogation room when Ross walked in.

"You have already been read your rights," said Ross as he sat down. "Let's not play with each other. Ima be real with you, and I want you to be real with me, so before you open your mouth to tell me a lie, let me advise you of a little fact. We got ya'll on tape with the murder of Cartoon. What can you tell me that will help you?" asked Ross.

Popeye just stared at him.

"Come on now, Popeye, give me something. What do you know about that church incident?" Ross asked.

"I don't know shit about shit," answered Popeye.

"Have it your way then," said Ross, "but for what we got you for, you will spend the rest of your life in a cell."

"Like I just told you, I don't know shit, so we can end this interview now," shot Popeye.

"So you would rather spend the rest of your life in a cell, beating your meat, while that pretty girl of yours starts fucking one of your homies?" Ross asked.

"Fuck you, Ross. I ain't telling you shit, and I don't have anything else to say!" yelled Popeye.

"No," said Ross in a calm voice. "Fuck your cellie. When you get upstate, he might be into that." Ross got up and walked out of the room and into the room where they had Hitman and found him with his head down on the table. "Praying ain't going to help you on this one," said Ross, taking a seat.

"I'm not praying. I'm tired as fuck," said Hitman, "so how about ya'll take me to a cell or let my ass go home?"

"So we can make this quick then, huh?" asked Ross.

Hitman just looked at him because he knew Ross was about to be on some bullshit.

"You and your boy," said Ross, "I got ya'll asses on tape the night ya'll gunned down Cartoon. Now you can play dumb and take your ass to prison with Popeye, or you can show me how smart you really are and help yourself out."

"How about ya'll show me to my bed?" said Hitman.

"Look, Hitman, give me some info on that church incident because we all know it was somebody from the Bottoms that did it. Three somebodies, actually," said Ross. "Don't be dumb. I can have you back on the streets within twelve years—fifteen, maybe—so just tell me what you know."

"What I know is that you are on some bullshit. Book me or let me go. I ain't got shit else to say," said Hitman.

"So you choose door number one," said Ross. "That's the dumb door, you fucking dumbass." Ross walked out of the room and told one of the uniformed officers to book both of them.

"What's the charges, sir?" asked the officer.

"First-degree murder," answered Ross over his shoulder as he walked away. Then he came back. "And put them in separate cells. I don't want them talking or seeing each other."

***

Cdog sat in the visiting room with Cooper, who had been coming to the prison twice a month just to pull him out to talk. Their relationship had grown into a kind of friendship. Cdog felt in his heart that Cooper really was on his side.

"Look," said Cooper as he was about to end their visit, "I'm leaving you this letter a guy I helped keep off death row wrote. He speaks about some very powerful stuff, and I want to share it with you. He is from Watts, California."

"Good looking, Coop," said Cdog. "Ima check it out as soon as I hit my cell."

"Until next time," said Cooper as he stood up to leave, giving Cdog the peace sign.

"Peace," Cdog said back to him.

A little while later, lying on his bunk, Cdog reached into his locker and pulled out the letter. He began reading it, and before he knew it, he was walking around the cell, reading out loud.

**We weaken and cripple ourselves with the way we move as a people, with no rules, no compassion for one another, and at times with no respect for ourselves. We are the strongest creation known to man. Our termination has been executed precisely as planned by the powers that be, but some way, somehow, we continue to exist. Their plan to rid us from Earth has failed, so as any smart person would do, they have resorted to having the strong kill the strong, black on black. But still, as a race, we prevail.**

**In my time and/or era, the most obvious move the powers that be made to display how much they feared and were intimidated by the black race was how they had purposely sabotaged the gang truce between the Crips and the Bloods. Then they not only allowed but also encouraged and financed the unification of the south-sider Mexicans. With the group of Warriors, Soldiers, Scholars, and Strategists, the gang truce was produced from both sides of the Crips and the Bloods. The entire country that we call America was put on high alert, knowing that an uprising would soon follow, not an**

uprising that caused violence, not unless violence was being forced upon us, but an uprising that would've held our best interest as a people, an interest that would've benefitted not only the black race but also mankind, period.

Just think of the inventions we as black people made while being oppressed, the work we have accomplished from being forced to do. Now allow these same people to think and work under humane conditions and see what production we would contribute to the world. We as black people define and motivate so much in the world without even trying to. From music, style, dance, beauty, these things come naturally to us, while for others, it takes a lifetime to learn and/or achieve. We are a race that's full of accomplishments that should be respected and looked upon as examples of success. What other group of people have displayed the strength we have in regards to being enslaved? We endured so much physically and mentally, but it was our spirituality that made us go on. From beatings, lynchings, denial of education, deprived of being a human, these are conditions that most races would succumb to before no longer existing.

I'm currently serving a life-without-parole sentence in prison, which most people would say contributed to how I think now as opposed to how I thought before I came here. In so many ways, they would be right. This place has not only forced me to be a man but also taught me how to be a black man, which was the key element of education I was lacking on the streets. I had no real self-pride as a black man, but I could tell you who, why, and when my neighborhood was started. I couldn't, back then, tell you who Marcus Garvey was, but I could tell you who Big Tookie or Raymond Washington was. I wasn't able to tell you what had happened to the black kids at that Little Rock School but was able to recall almost every gang fight that went down at my junior and/or high school. Before coming to prison, I didn't know the name of the first ship carrying slaves from Africa to America, but I could, however, tell you who had the biggest rims on their car in the hood. I have allowed "them" to entrap me once again into physical slavery, prison, but we as a people are not paying attention to the mental slavery they are pushing on us, which consists of drugs, welfare, and miseducation, all things set up to not only keep us stuck in the hood (plantation) but also keep our minds from advancing.

The United States education system is so blatant with their tactics until people can't see them. The surest way in this day and the future to get a nice-paying career is to be bilingual. Every other race is being taught English, giving them bilingual status, but our kids are not mandated to learn a second language, so they are not being taught one, which cripples our kids' future and may hold them back from a nice and secure future. Plus, this process eliminates proper communication with other races, thus limiting our interaction to ourselves.

Although they (Mexicans) have declared themselves our mortal enemy, I must say that I respect their outlook on discipline. No one is too big to receive punishment for violating their rules. We (blacks), on the other hand, have been tricked to pacify and protect those who provide us with material and/or monetary items regardless of what they may have done and, in some cases, what they haven't done. For any movement to be successful, there must be rules adhered to at all times, and violation of these rules must be met with the necessary punishment, sometimes even resulting in death, but in no case can anyone be exempt from discipline for violating a rule. Sometimes the masses of the movement actually need to see someone being punished for a violation. The higher rank the person is in the organization, the better.

Everyone must understand that yes, we reward those who are loyal to the movement but won't hesitate to have your head for any violation that calls for it.

Regardless of what you may bring to the table—money, weapons, or the ability to use your brain—never think you are bigger than the movement. Don't get the gangs of today confused with what a movement is. Gangs may have been started as something to be a part of to help keep our community safe from outsiders, but that concept has been replaced with us killing one another, childhood friends and sometimes even family members resorting to gunfire against one another, resulting in hate and envy for the people who once shared a bowl of cereal together while watching cartoons. This act has separated and destroyed many communities. It left us vulnerable and blind to the many areas that required our attention. Seeing the lack of our focus allowed things like the drugs, snitches, undercover agents, etc. to be planted in our neighborhoods. Other than the dependency of welfare, which broke us down, now drugs have taken the will, the heart, the courage, and the life itself from most of the black community. The bomb they dropped on us called drugs has left us in a state of mind that can only be described as the shock-and-awe tactic. These drugs have made it easy to forget that your child isn't receiving a proper education. They make it easy for a father or mother to abandon their kids. They make it easy to be content with welfare. But the most important reason to the people who had dropped this bomb on us was for us as a race to forget how to fight, and it's working. When you can't rid yourself of your enemy physically, then you must do it mentally, but to do this, you must become them, which means do as he does, think as he thinks. For us blacks, there have been many attempts from various races to rid us from Earth, but thus far, every attempt has failed because it was directed more on physical termination, which was met with powerful resistance. Now they are trying to overtake us with the mental approach. They have learned our language, our music, our food, our dress code, our every way of life, and they are slowly making it their own. If you don't believe this process is taking place, then I ask you to take a moment and about how the person who claimed they hated you five, ten, or fifteen years ago because of your skin color. Now they look, sound, and try to act just like you. It's the classic saying that goes, "If you can't beat 'em, then join 'em." Our enemies have been gathering intel on us for years, and now they are starting to use this information. What's even crazier is that there are some blacks who have the means of making our people aware through TV and/or radio of this plot, yet they remain silent. I was watching a TV show the other day, and they made a comment that supports my theory. They said that in the coming years, mixed races will be the next black race because of all the blacks having kids with other races.

"Damn. This is some powerful shit," said Cdog as he laid the letter down and thought about what he had just read. "And this is from the mind of a dude in prison," he said out loud to himself. "There's some smart muthafuckas behind bars." Cdog picked the letter back up and started rereading certain parts. This dude held Cdog's interest and had him holding onto every word. Cdog's mind was really feeling this dude. "I need to step my game up with my reading and awareness," Cdog said as he got up and cut his cell light off and then went to bed.

*** Popeye walked to the phone in the holding tank and dialed Tonya's number. He knew as soon as she had answered the phone that she was crying. "Hello," Popeye said, but Tonya didn't say anything back. She just cried. "I'm sure you know what they got me for, but—"

"*Murder!*" Tonya screamed, cutting him off. "I can't believe you did this shit to us, Popeye."

"Baby, we gon' get through this," said Popeye.

"How the fuck we gon' do that?" Tonya asked. "Nigga, you can't hug me late night from no fucking jail cell!" she hollered.

"Baby, just trust me, okay," said Popeye but feeling like he had already lost Tonya.

"I already trusted you, and look, Popeye. Look where that got me!" she shouted into the phone.

Popeye couldn't say anything because she was speaking the truth.

"That's what I thought, nigga. Get quiet. I can't do it, Popeye," Tonya said. "I'm sorry, but I just can't do it."

"So you just gonna walk away and leave me stuck like this?" Popeye asked.

"I'm at our home, where I'm supposed to be you, the one who ain't," answered Tonya. "I need to lie down, Popeye. You got my head hurting from all this bullshit."

"Tonya, you know you all I got. I need you more than ever right now," pleaded Popeye.

"Then you should've thought of that when you was out here doing the shit that got you there. I will always love you, but I can't do this. Bye, Popeye. I wish you the best," she said, and she hung up the phone.

"Tonya!" Popeye yelled into the phone. "Tonya!" But there was no response. He just stood there with the phone to his ear, wishing that what had just happened wasn't real. "*Fuck, fuck, fuck, fuck!*" he screamed while hitting the phone with the receiver. He sat on the bench next to the phone, looking like he was waiting on it to ring, and that was when Ross's voice popped into his head, saying, "Your homie going to be fucking that pretty girl of yours."

Three days later, Popeye and Hitman were escorted to court, and they pled not guilty. Their bail was set at four million dollars, which meant they both would be sitting in the county jail awaiting trial. Popeye did a quick scan of the courtroom seats looking for Tonya, but she was a no-show. On the ride to the county jail, Popeye was handcuffed to an old dude who couldn't stop talking.

"You see, youngsta," the old dude said, "the county jail is the mouth of hell. Everything gotta go through the mouth to get to the stomach, which is what we call prison. Every so often, the stomach need to make room for the new stuff being shoved into the mouth, so the stomach shits, and that's called parole, but some of the stuff remain in the stomach, and that's called doing life in hell."

"Do me a favor, OG," said Popeye.

"What's that, youngsta?" asked the old dude.

"Shut the fuck up," answered Popeye.

*** Tank was on the yard working when he heard his name over the loudspeaker saying for him to report back to the building and see the counselor. *Damn,* thought Tank as he walked across the yard. *What the fuck is this about?* The incident in the kitchen bathroom popped into his head. Tank was let into the building and walked to the counselor's office but had to wait because another inmate was already inside. Tank stood behind the out-of-bounds line painted on the floor and waited. *This better not be about that homosexual 'cause if it is, Ima beat his ass again, and Ima beat Porsche's ass for telling me I had nothing to worry about,* thought Tank.

The other dude walked out of the office, and Tank went to the door.

"You call for Adams?" asked Tank.

"Yeah, come on in, Mr. Adams," said the counselor. "Close the door behind you."

Tank walked in and closed the door and sat in the chair across from the counselor.

"I'm CC2 Jones, and I got some papers for you to fill out and sign," she said.

"What kind of papers?" asked Tank.

"Walking papers. It's time to do your parole plans," answered Jones.

Tank's heart skipped a beat as a big-ass smile came across his face.

"I need the address to where you plan on staying. Then I need you to sign here and here," said Jones, pointing, "but first, read everything because these are your parole conditions."

Tank's hand shook as he picked up the papers. He read them quickly and signed his name, declaring he would follow the conditions and that he understood them.

"Okay, on this paper, I need your address," said Ms. Jones.

Tank filled in his mom's address.

"Who will you be living with?" she asked Tank.

"My mother," Tank answered.

"Write her name here," Jones said, and she pointed.

Tank did as she had asked and then handed her back the paperwork.

"Your release date will be within the next three to five months, so try to keep out of trouble until then," Ms. Jones said.

"So right after the summer, I should be gone?" Tank asked.

"I think you may be able to catch a week or two of the summer," Jones said with a smile.

"That would be nice," Tank shot back.

"Good luck, Mr. Adams, and stay out of places like this," she told Tank.

"Oh, I will. Thank you." Tank walked out of the office a happy man and went straight to the phone, where he called Lisa. "Hello," he said once she had accepted.

"Hey, baby," she said, sounding clogged up.

"Damn, why you sound like that?" Tank asked.

"Because I'm fighting off a cold," lied Lisa. She didn't want to tell him Nesha had broken her nose.

"I hope my baby get well soon," he said. "Aye, I got some news for you."

"I hope it's better than the news I got for you," said Lisa.

"I signed my parole papers," he said as if he hadn't heard her last comment.

"You did? For real, Tank?" she asked, excited.

"Yep. I'm about to be up outta this muthafucka," he answered.

"I can't wait," Lisa said. "Shit, after your news, I hate to tell you my news."

"The way I feel right now, almost nothing can bring me down," said Tank. "What is it?"

"Ross got Popeye and Hitman a few days ago. They sitting in the county jail," said Lisa.

"Oh yeah? What, they catch them niggas with a gun or some dope?" Tank asked.

"Naw," said Lisa. "First-degree murder."

"What?" Tank yelled, which made a few dudes in the dayroom look his way.

"Murder, Tank," Lisa said again.

"I heard you the first fucking time," Tank said. "Murder on who?"

"Nobody know yet, but they was doing all types of wild shit out here. I'm shocked it's only on murder," said Lisa.

"Don't talk like that," said Tank, knowing their call may be getting recorded, which made him wrap the call up. "I love you and will call back soon."

"I love you too," said Lisa.

"Take some medicine," Tank said as he hung up the phone.

*** Nesha couldn't take it anymore. She had been gone from Lisa's house for almost two weeks. All she thought about was her niece. *I got to be there for her 'cause ain't no telling what Lisa doing or who she laid up with right* *now*. Nesha drove the few blocks to Lisa's house from the motel she was staying in. She noticed Lisa's car in the driveway when she pulled up. "At least the bitch at home," mumbled Nesha to herself as she parked her car and went to the door, where she let herself in.

She stopped in her tracks as she looked around the living room. It was a mess. Shit was knocked over. Clothes and dirty dishes were all over the floor. Lisa hadn't even cleaned up the blood from their fight. "This a nasty bitch," said Nesha. It hurt her heart to know that her niece was forced to live like this. Nesha walked to Lisa's bedroom and found her asleep in the bed with some kind of mask on her face. "Lisa," said Nesha, standing next to the bed. "Wake your ass up."

Lisa began to move and rolled over to face Nesha. "You broke my nose," Lisa said to her sister with pain in her voice.

Nesha just looked at her.

"I didn't deserve this, Nesha. You of all people know I didn't mean any of the things I said to you." Lisa started crying. "I'm so sorry, sis. I didn't mean any of it."

Pity began to take over the anger Nesha had felt, and she sat down on the bed next to her big sister.

"I know my life is a mess right now," said Lisa, "but I swear I'm trying to get my shit together. I can't do it without your help though."

Those words broke Nesha all the way down, and she began to cry. "I'm sorry too, Lisa," Nesha said, and then she threw her arms around her sister.

They hugged each other and cried for thirty minutes.

"I'm coming back home," said Nesha.

"Please do," replied Lisa as she looked at her sister.

"But, bitch, first, we need to clean this muthafucka up," said Nesha, and they both laughed.

"It ain't that bad," said Lisa, looking around.

"So you don't smell that funk all through the house?" asked Nesha.

"Bitch, I haven't smelled shit since you hit me with that uppercut," answered Lisa.

"I'm sorry for that," said Nesha, feeling bad for doing it.

"I know you are, and I forgive you. Shit, low-key, I needed that ass whipping. It made me realize how bad I was fucking up. Plus, this nose took me to the hospital, and while there, I had some test done," lied Lisa.

"Okay, so what they say?" asked Nesha.

"That I'm in perfect health and all I need is some rest." Lisa told her sister that lie and actually believed it herself. She didn't have one test run on her.

"I got some weed in the car," said Nesha.

They spent the next four hours cleaning, smoking, and catching each other up on the latest gossip.

"So Tank signed his parole papers, huh?" said Nesha, happy for her sister.

"Yep, my baby on his way home," replied Lisa "I can't wait."

"Things are falling back in line for you, so you gotta stay on point and continue to remain focused. Fuck all that dumb shit," said Nesha. "So trip. That weed got a bitch hungry. Let's go get something to eat."

"I'm not going outside looking like this," said Lisa, pointing at her mask. "Order a pizza."

"Okay, pizza, it is." Nesha was happy to be back home. She was even happier to have the old Lisa back. "I love you, sis."

"I more love you," replied Lisa, and she meant every word.

*** The first few weeks of living in the county jail were hard for Popeye. It seemed like every day someone new would pop up at his cell door, claiming to be one of Cartoon's homies and how they needed that. So he gave that to them, winning some and losing some, but he fought every day. Even when his body said no, he threw his dukes up, all until his OG homie named Happy landed in his module.

"What's the deal, lil homie?" asked Happy, standing on the tier for chow.

"What it do, big homie?" replied Popeye with a big-ass black eye.

"I heard you was over here, so I had to come check on you. I'm the trustee for this floor now, but what's popping with that eye, nigga?" asked Happy.

"Niggas been coming at me left and right behind that Cartoon shit," answered Popeye.

"Is that right?" said Happy. "Oh, we gon' put a stop to that. Let me finish passing out these trays, and Ima be back. Where your boy Hitman?"

"They got him on the new side," Popeye said.

"Y'all ain't keep away, are ya'll?" asked Happy.

"Naw, we good," answered Popeye.

"Give me his name, and I'll have my boy move him in here after chow," Happy said, looking around Popeye's cell and seeing the empty bunk.

Popeye wrote Hitman's name on some paper and then handed it to Happy. "I don't know his booking number," said Popeye.

"This all I need right here," replied Happy.

"They got you for that robbery?" asked Popeye.

"Yeah, they trying to give me twenty-two years for that punk shit because of my past," answered Happy, and he shook his head.

"They ain't playing with no nigga," said Popeye, which made them both laugh.

"Naw, they ain't," said Happy, "but trip, I got something special for you. Ima bring it when I come back. I should have your boy over here by tonight. Let me finish with these dinner trays, and I'll holla back when I'm done."

"Yep, fo' sho'," said Popeye as Happy moved down the tier with the trays.

Popeye sat down on his bunk and ate his food. By the time he had finished, Happy was back at the cell door.

"That move is good. He should be packing his shit right now," said Happy. "Here, nigga. Fuck all that playing with these bustas." He handed Popeye a nine-inch ice pick with the handle and tip already on it. "The next one of them fools that push up on you, put some holes in his ass, and I hope I'm on the tier."

"Good looking, big homie," said Popeye, feeling like he was back on the block with his gun.

"You know how real Bottoms niggas do. We all we got," said Happy.

"Bottoms up," said Popeye, and they both laughed.

"If you need something else, let me know. I'm in the trustee cell around the corner," said Happy.

"Fo' sho', big dog, and good looking again on this," said Popeye.

"Shit, you may as well get some practice in now so when you hit that big house, you will be ready," replied Happy. "Niggas don't really do the fistfight thang up there. They play with iron."

Popeye had a few questions about prison or the big house, as Happy called it, but kept them for later.

"Ima holla later tonight," said Happy as he walked off.

"Yep!" yelled Popeye back at him, and then he sat on his bunk.

Popeye lay back and closed his eyes, but just when it felt like he was about to go to sleep, the cell door began to open. He jumped off the bunk with the pick in his hand and stuck his head out the open door. Walking down the tier toward him was Hitman.

"Bottoms, nigga," said Popeye with a big smile on his face.

"Oh, so I see they gave a Bottom nigga some juice," said Hitman, laughing. As he got closer, he saw Popeye's eye. "What the fuck happen to your eye?" Hitman asked, yelling.

"Calm down, nigga. I had a few suckas push up on me," answered Popeye.
"They rat-pack you?" asked Hitman.

"Naw, every day a new nigga seem to pop up at the door, talking about
he need that, so I been fighting my ass off. One of them niggas caught me
with a few good ones," answered Popeye.

"I hope they bitch ass ready to line it up again!" Hitman yelled over the
tier so the whole module could hear. "On Bottoms!"

"The big homie Happy came through today and saved me this." Popeye
handed the ice pick to Hitman. "He the one that got you moved over here."

"Yeah, this nice right here. He gon' have to hit me with one," said Hitman.
"Who all here?"

"Me, you, and Happy," said Popeye. "That fool Happy is a trustee."

They spent the rest of the night talking about the latest hood news.

"I'm telling you, they said Nesha beat Lisa's ass," said Hitman.

"Naw, I would've heard about that," said Popeye.

"Man, broke that bitch's nose and some more shit," Hitman said, and
they laughed.

"Ima call her when I get up," said Popeye, turning on his bunk to face the
wall. "I'm gone, my nigga. I'll holla in the morning, fool. Bottoms."

"Bottoms," replied Hitman.

*** Cdog didn't know what to say to the shit Cooper was telling him. Today
was another one of those dry runs to court, which had Cdog steaming hot.

"The DA said they are willing to give us two, maybe three more months
to take their offer, or they plan to move ahead on your case," said Cooper.

Cdog still hadn't spoken.

"So at some point, you need to let me know what we're doing," finished
Cooper.

"What we doing?" asked Cdog with anger in his voice. "We ain't doing
shit. I'm the one who will be doing time, so don't give me that 'we' shit."

Frustration was starting to set in on Cooper. *After bending over backward
for this dude, this is how he repays me*, thought Cooper.

"You know what? You're right. You will be the one doing time, just like
you are the fucking one who decided to take that c/o's life, so I'm sorry I
wasn't there to help, but don't you dare try to make me feel guilty for your
fuck-up," said Cooper. "I told you up front that my job was trying to keep you
off death row, and you better believe me when I tell you that's where you're

going due to the evidence they got against you. So throw all the pity parties and guilt trips you want, but at the end of the day, when you lie down, please remember it was your choice that put you in this situation. I'm trying to save your life, but if you feel it ain't worth saving, then I'm wasting my fucking time on your case." Cooper laid it all on the table for Cdog. He was tired of feeling like he was the one who had committed a crime.

They sat for a few minutes in total silence, and then Cdog spoke.

"My bad, Coop. I was outta line for what I said, and I apologize for it," said Cdog. "Just give me a little more time to think about what I need to do."

*Damn, this young dude keeps reminding me of my little brother*, thought Cooper. "I will stall this case as long as I can, but after so long, I won't be able to so. I just hope for your sake, it ain't too late," said Cooper.

"You will have my answer soon," Cdog replied.

"That's good to know," said Cooper. "So did you read the letter I gave you?"

"Of course, I did. That's some powerful stuff. He really opened my eyes to a few things I never paid attention to," answered Cdog.

"Yeah, he was special and didn't realize it," said Cooper.

"What you mean 'was'? You stop him from going to death row, right?" asked Cdog.

"Yes, I was able to get him life without parole in prison, but he was too political to be trapped inside a place designed for the purpose of oppressing people," Cooper said, sounding sad and proud at the same time. "The c/os set him up to be killed by some white inmates who later testified against the c/os, who are now serving prison terms. The family was paid some nice money from the state, but all that knowledge and passion he had was buried with him. That's why I cherish those letters."

"So ya'll became friends before he died?" asked Cdog.

"Naw," answered Cooper, standing up to leave. "He was my little brother." Cooper walked off, leaving Cdog with no chance to say anything.

Now back in his cell, Cdog thought hard about his life and finally made up his mind on what he needed to do, so he pulled out his paper and pen and began a letter to Cooper.

> First and foremost, let me extend my sorrow for the loss of
> your brother. Just from me reading his letters, I know he
> was a solid man. I also would like to say I appreciate the

friendship you and I have come to know. Since our last visit, I've been sitting back, reflecting on my life. It's been hard to accept some of the decisions I have made. It's so hard because some of those decisions were so juvenile, and as a grown man, I should not have made them. I should've been more aware of my actions because of the experiences I've endured throughout my life leading up to that one moment. It's funny in a crazy kind of way how we equip ourselves with knowledge but then allow one second to erase all we have learned. Most people would call that one second being caught up in the moment, but shouldn't that be the moment when all your knowledge kicks in and tells you to stop, "Don't do that"? After all the struggles I've been through and all the knowledge I've obtained, I still became vulnerable to my surroundings. My desire to be hood famous made me think as a child. Today I'm faced with a grown-man decision, and as a grown man, I'm ready to accept the consequences for my actions. Thinking like a grown man, I realize to take this case to trial, I would be fighting a war I stand no chance at winning. Thank you, my friend, for helping to save my life, although it will be spent locked forever in hell.

***

Popeye was laid back on his bunk in thought as Hitman took a quick nap.

Happy, who was grooming them for prison life, had told them, "At no time during the day should both of ya'll be asleep. One up, one down. Somebody need to be on guard at all times."

Popeye followed Happy's instructions from the moment he had heard them, and with doing so, he was able to see the dude who had just walked by their cell. Popeye didn't think too much of it at first until the dude walked by the second time and was looking in the cell.

"Aye, what's up, homie?" asked Popeye, jumping up off his bunk. "You looking for somebody?"

"Yeah, I'm looking for a nigga named Popeye," answered the dude.

Hitman instantly sat up out of his sleep and put his shoes on.

"You looking for Popeye?" Popeye asked the dude.

"That's what I said, nigga," replied the dude, and it made Popeye smile.

"I'm Popeye, homie. What you looking for me for?" he asked, but he already knew the answer.

"Nigga, don't play dumb. You know what time it is," said the dude. "Ima need that when this door come open."

"You need what?" asked Happy, who had crept down the tier unnoticed.

"This between me and him," said the dude to Happy, not knowing he was from the Bottoms.

"Oh, you trying to get in this cell?" asked Happy, pointing. "I can get it open for you."

"That's what's up," said the dude.

Happy walked back toward the front with a smile on his face, knowing that his boy was at work and would open any door for him. Popeye walked to the back of the cell and felt a little nervous about what was going to take place. He had never stabbed anyone before but knew this nigga was going to be the first. Popeye glanced at Hitman and hunched his shoulders as if to say, "Ima give this nigga what he want." Hitman nodded. The door to the cell opened, and the dude ran in toward Popeye and started swinging haymakers. Popeye ducked under the punches and hit the dude twice in the side with the ice pick.

The dude stopped swinging and took a few steps back and then said, "Naw, nigga. We ain't going body." Then he took a glance at Popeye's hands and saw the weapon. He tried to back out of the cell, but Happy was at the door by then.

"Where you going, nigga?" asked Happy as he pushed the dude back toward Popeye. "This what you wanted, right?"

The dude realized that he had walked into the lion's den as Hitman jumped off the bunk and hit him from the back, knocking him to the ground.

"Y'all go to work on this clown-ass nigga," said Happy, and he watched as Popeye put hole after hole in the dude's body.

"I'm not playing with you niggas," said Popeye as the ice pick entered the dude. "Fuck that nigga Cartoon." *Stab.* "Fuck you." *Stab.* "Fuck your set." *Stab, stab, stab.* Blood was all over the cell floor as the dude just lay there, balled up.

"That's enough," said Happy as he grabbed Popeye, who had a demonic look on his face. "Ima drag this nigga to his cell. Y'all start cleaning up." Happy first went and got the dude's cell door open and then dragged him out of Popeye and Hitman's cell. Happy knew that the ice pick had hit some vital organs, and the dude wasn't going to make it. He put the nigga in his bunk, threw a blanket over him like he was sleeping, and walked out back to Popeye's cell.

"You straight?" Hitman asked Popeye when they were alone.

"Yeah, I'm good," replied Popeye while thinking he was never having another fistfight.

Two days later, the police discovered the dude's lifeless body in the cell.

"Bottoms," said Popeye, laid back on his bunk.

\*\*\*

For the last couple of weeks, Junebug felt good. He was back to working out every day, and he wasn't being haunted by memories of Lisa. He couldn't remember the exact day, but he had even taken down the photo of her taped to the top bunk and put it inside one of his letters. He and his little brother were back on the right track after Junebug had sent him a letter and apologized for taking his anger out on him. *The old Junebug is back and better than ever,* he thought as he looked into the cell mirror. *I been straight tripping. I need to get this SHU over with and get my ass back to the main line so I can at least start doing the things the board require to go home.*

But then just like snapping your fingers, something went off inside Junebug's head that made him return to feeling depressed. "Ima die in prison," Junebug said to himself as he began to pace the floor of his cell. "I need you, Lisa," he mumbled, and memories of her once again took over his mind. He saw them holding hands and laughing. He saw the day their daughter, Mercedes, was born. He saw them making love. The images that flashed through his mind were more than he could take. He fell to the floor of his cell and cried like a baby. "Why, Lisa?" he asked out loud. "Why are you doing this to us?"

Junebug once again had fallen into the state of mind where his every thought was about Lisa. All he wanted was his Lisa. Nothing else mattered. He grabbed the letter her photo was in and pulled out the picture. In it, she had a smile on her face that melted Junebug's heart. "I love you," he said to the photo. "I really, really love you."

\*\*\* Two months had gone by, and Cdog hadn't seen or heard from Cooper until today. Cdog sat chained up in the court holding tank, listening to what his lawyer was saying.

"After our last visit, I flew to California and spent some time at my brother's grave site. I needed to get some things off my mind," said Cooper.

"That's understandable," replied Cdog.

"No, you don't understand," shot Cooper. "I was the one who convinced him to take that plea deal. He wanted to go to death row and be executed. He said that he didn't want to live his remaining days on Earth with people telling him what he could or couldn't do. I thought he was just on another political war trip, so I pushed him hard to take that deal, and for what? He was still killed by the system."

"You starting to confuse me," said Cdog.

Cooper took a long look at Cdog before saying, "Look, I don't want to make the same mistake I made with my brother. I should've let that choice be his to make, which brings me to you. Yes, if you take this case to trial, I'm pretty sure you will end up on death row, and I personally don't want to see you there, but it's your choice from here on out how this case proceeds."

"I've made up my mind," said Cdog. "I'm not ready to die. Although prison life is hard, I will at least still be alive. I'm already serving a life sentence, so won't be too much change for me if they added another one. I'm ready to take the deal, and whatever happens to me along the way won't be on anyone but me."

"As you said in the letter you sent to me, that's some grown-man thinking. A smart grown man, if I may add," said Cooper.

"So when do we get this shit done?" asked Cdog.

"It won't happen today, but I'll start the process," answered Cooper. "I will be up to the prison soon. Peace, my brother." Cooper gave Cdog the black power fist.

"Peace," said Cdog, and without thinking, he gave the fist back to Cooper as he walked away.

Sitting on his bunk back in the cell, Cdog was deep in thought. One side of him was asking if he really wanted to spend the rest of his life inside an average-size bathroom with people telling him what to do—when to eat, when to shower, and when to go outside. *Yeah*, said the voice in his head, *you may be breathing, but you won't be living. This prison shit ain't living.* But the other side of him was saying, *At least with breath in your body, you still got hope. You keep the opportunity to see your mom's face. You will be able to remain in the lives of your loved ones. Don't let them people take that from you by allowing them to kill you.*

Cdog stood up from his bunk and walked to the mirror hanging over his sink. He looked at himself for about two minutes before saying out loud, "I wanna keep living. I got unfinished business to tend to."

\*\*\* Time for Tank seemed to be moving at a snail's pace. The days were longer, and it took next to forever for a week to go by. Tank tried anything and everything to stay busy. He worked out four, sometimes five hours a day. Plus, he had a yard crew job, but not even all that activity during the day helped him sleep at night. He would lie on his bunk for hours wide awake, thinking about what the future held for him. He knew that Cdog, if he already hadn't, would send the paperwork on him to the hood, and now that Popeye was in jail, there was no one left he could team up with if or when shit got ugly. *Ima have to be low-key as fuck*, thought Tank.

"Them young niggas coming up in the hood would be happy to get these stripes for killing the Tank," he mumbled. *Or if I knock down one of them, this what I'm coming back to because I can never hit another main line.* Then the reality of his situation hit him hard when he realized that he had no other place to go except the hood when he got out. *I got to make a few dollars in the hood just to get out the hood*, thought Tank, *and there's no way of doing that without niggas knowing.* Tank rolled over on his side and faced the wall. He knew that his life was on borrowed time after the stunt he had pulled on Cdog, but he hadn't thought about all the consequences he may encounter. *I only thought about having to deal with Cdog and straight overlooked the fact that I went against the code of the streets, and once you do that, you become fair game to anyone. I should've kept my shit gangsta and stuck my knife in Cdog. At least then, I would only have to worry about him.*

Tank closed his eyes and finally drifted off to sleep, but when he awoke, the same thoughts haunted him. "Let me get my ass up and ready for work," Tank said to himself as his feet hit the floor. Two hours later, Tank was pushing a cart from building to building, collecting the bags of trash. He hated this job also, but it wasn't the kitchen, so he dealt with it. When he got to the last building, he heard his name over the loudspeaker telling him to report back to his block.

"What the fuck?" he asked out loud as he turned and went back to his building.

"You got a visit," the tower cop said, looking out the back window.

"A visit on a Tuesday?" asked Tank.

"Must be an attorney visit," said the c/o as he opened the door to let Tank in so he could get dressed.

*Fuck an attorney coming to see me for?* Tank asked himself as he walked to his cell. Ten minutes later, Tank found himself sitting in the visiting room at a table with two private investigators.

"I'm PI Garcia, and this is PI Lopez," said the short fat one with the thick-ass mustache. "We are here on behalf of the district attorney office, and we need to ask you a few questions."

"Questions about what?" Tank played dumb.

"This is the tape that was made by a prison captain interviewing you about the murder of a correctional officer, and this is everything on the tape written down," said Lopez, and he pointed to the folder.

"We would like you to read the statement before we go any further," said Garcia.

Tank spent the next thirty-five minutes reading the paperwork and then set it back on the table.

"Okay, now our questions are simple ones," said Garcia. "The first question is did you make these statements?"

Tank hesitated for a moment before saying with his head down, "Yes, I did."

"Is there anything you want to add or take out from this statement?"

Tank answered with one word. "No."

"So under penalty of perjury, you stand by your account of the crime?" Garcia asked.

"Yes, I do" came from Tank.

"And if called to testify, you will?"

"Yes, I will," Tank said.

"Then all we need is your signature, and we done here," said Lopez as he passed Tank a pen and the papers. "Sign here, here, and here." Lopez pointed to the three spots.

Tank signed his name and then got up from the table and signaled the c/o that he was ready to return to the yard.

*** "Yo, it might go down with these Mexicans at roof time. One of the black trustees beat the shit outta one in the laundry room when they came back from court," said Happy. "Y'all take these." Happy handed them two knives.

"What the Mexicans saying?" asked Popeye, grabbing the weapons through the cell bars.

"They ain't said shit, and that alone should have a nigga on alert," said Happy. "I got to go let a few other dudes know the business."

"Okay, big homie. We will be ready," said Hitman as Happy walked off.

"When these fucking Mexicans gon' learn they can't fuck with niggas?" asked Popeye.

"Shit, them some dumb muthafuckas. They just don't seem to learn," answered Hitman.

"Yeah, I see," said Popeye. "Ima try to kill me one if the shit kick off."

"I hear you, my boy," replied Hitman, who was examining his weapon. "This muthafucka right here is nice." He stabbed at the air and laughed.

"That fool Happy is some kind of pro putting these together," said Popeye.

"Charlie and Denver rows, get ready for roof time," said the police over the speaker.

The roof was where they had a handball and basketball court, phones, and vending machines. It was also the only place other than going to court where inmates could see the sky and smell the fresh air.

"Watch the doors. Doors are opening," said the police as the doors began to open.

Popeye and Hitman stepped onto the tier with their knives between their ass cheeks. One of them looked left down the tier, while the other one looked right. They let the back part of the tier walk by them before they fell in line. Once on the roof, the line separated, with the Mexicans going to one side and the blacks to the other side. Tension was in the air.

"Shit, do we wait to see what they wanna do, or do we take it to them?" Hitman asked Happy.

"Just give it a minute or two. If it's going down, then it's gon' happen" said Happy as he un-cheeked his knife. "You two niggas stay with me, and no matter what, don't fall."

"Yep," Hitman and Popeye said at the same time.

"They always got us outnumbered, but them fools can't fight," said Happy. "They can kick though, and that's why you gotta stay on your feet. You hit that ground, it's ova."

Two Mexicans broke away from their pack and walked halfway to where the blacks were and then motioned for Happy to check it out.

"They don't want any problems. They wanna talk," Happy told the blacks. "Y'all come with me," he said to Popeye and Hitman.

"Aye, what's up, Happy?" said a Mexican named Trigger. "This my homie Joker, ay."

"Yep, these my little homies, Popeye and Hitman," said Happy.

Then everybody shook hands.

"Aye, homes, on behalf of my people, we want to apologize for the disrespect that fool displayed. Your people had every right to handle his business, and from me to you, we don't wanna have things go beyond what already happened," said Trigger.

"I feel you on that, and I'm sure my people are willing to leave that shit alone as well. Your boy was all the way in the wrong," replied Happy.

"We got a couple youngstas who will be dealing with him for that," said Trigger.

"Then we all good, fool?" asked Happy.

"Yep, and, Happy, you know anytime one of your people have a problem with one of mine, holla at me, and I'll get that shit handled, my boy," answered Trigger.

"Fo' sho'," said Happy. "Y'all enjoy some of this fresh air."

"Likewise, fool," said Trigger, and everyone shook hands again.

"That shit over, ya'll," Happy said to the blacks when he walked up. "Popeye, you and Hitman keep ya'll eyes open. You can never trust a dope fiend."

They all laughed.

*Damn*, thought Popeye as he walked away from the crowd, *I won't be able to have any fun with my tool today*. Popeye reached the phone and dialed Tonya's number. His heartbeat sped up when he heard her answer, but anger took over him when he heard the recording say that the called party refused to accept the charges. Popeye put the phone back on the hook. "Punk-ass bitch," he said to himself. "I won't call your ass again." *I refuse to be the nigga walking around this muthafucka, stressing and tripping over a bitch*, Popeye thought as he caught up with Hitman. "The bitch wouldn't accept the charges."

"That's fucked up. You cool?" asked Hitman.

"Ima be all right, my boy. Ain't nothing I can do about the situation," Popeye answered.

"And that's the Bottom line," said Hitman, throwing up their hood sign, laughing.

"Bottom line," Popeye said while throwing up the Bottom gang sign. "Fuck that bitch."

\*\*\* Cdog had tossed and turned all night from thinking about what he was going to do today. "This my last court run," he said to himself as he got dressed. "I have no choice but to accept the plea deal they offering me, and it's all because of that bitch-ass nigga Tank."

"Aye, Johnson, you about ready?" asked the c/o standing at the cell door.

"I'm ready when you are," answered Cdog.

"Then let's get the show on the road," said the c/o as he opened up the tray slot.

Cdog walked to the door and went along with the ritual of being placed in chains and cuffs. The ride to court seemed longer today than usual to Cdog as he looked out the window at the free world and saw people doing what they may very well do every day without even thinking about how precious it was to be able to come and go as you feel. The van pulled to the back of the court building and was let into the loading and unloading area for inmates. Cdog was taken inside and placed in a holding tank. Two hours later, the police opened the door and told Cdog it was time to go upstairs. They escorted him out to the hallway, where, just like all the other times he had been to court, there were about eight policemen waiting. Cdog was loaded onto the elevator and, after a few seconds, was being escorted to another holding tank.

"Your attorney will be back here soon," said one of the officers as he closed the door.

Cdog began to pace the floor of the holding tank, wishing this shit could be over with. "I'm so cool on all these court trips," he mumbled to himself. Cdog heard keys jingling, and the tank door opened.

"Your lawyer is here," said the officer.

"Good morning, Mr. Johnson," said Cooper, standing on the other side of the tank.

"Aye, what's up, Coop?" asked Cdog.

"So you know why you here, but let me ask anyway. Are you ready to proceed with your request?"

"Yeah, I'm ready," Cdog answered.

"Okay, they will call us into the courtroom shortly, and the judge will reread the charge against you. Then he will go into you having the right to a trial and a few other things. He's gonna say that a plea deal was reached. Then he will ask if you understand," said Cooper as Cdog nodded. "He will then go into if anyone pressured you to plead guilty and so on. Once all that is done, he will ask the state how much time they agreed to, and then he will ask you if that's what you signed for and if you are ready to be sentenced today."

"Okay, I understand," said Cdog.

"Personally," said Cooper, looking Cdog in the eye, "I think you doing the right thing."

"I think so too," said Cdog. "It may be a fucked-up choice, but it's the best one."

"Let me go see when they will be ready for us," said Cooper, and he walked out of the tank.

*This is it,* thought Cdog, sitting in the tank alone. *I made them fight me the first time they gave me life, but I'm taking life this time.*

"Johnson, they ready for you," said the bailiff.

Everything Cooper said the judge would say, he said.

"How do you plead to this charge?" asked the judge after everything else.

"Guilty," said Cdog.

"Let the record show that the defendant pleads guilty to the charge of murder. The court will accept that," said the judge. "Is there any reason for the sentence be delayed?"

"No, Your Honor," chimed Cooper and the DA.

"Young man, you have avoided the death penalty by pleading guilty, and I will accept the state recommendation of life without the possibility of parole," said the judge, and just like that, Cdog escaped death row but was sentenced to doing the rest of his life in hell.

*** Nesha had been back home for over a month, and her sister stood true to her word. She wasn't out all hours of the night, and Nesha hadn't seen one nigga pick her up from the house, but tonight Lisa had plans. Her money was getting low from being laid up the last two months.

"So you hitting the town, huh?" asked Nesha as she watched Lisa get dressed.

"Just for a few hours. I been cramped up in this house too long," answered Lisa.

Nesha hit her with another question. "Where you going?"

"I haven't really decided," lied Lisa, who already had a room booked at the hotel.

"You been doing good, sis. I hope you ain't falling back to your old ways," said Nesha.

Remembering the outcome of her last confrontation with Nesha, Lisa chose her words wisely this time. "Naw, little sis. I just need to stretch my legs for a few hours and have some fun," said Lisa as she looked up at Nesha, hoping she was buying her story, but it was obvious Nesha wasn't convinced because she pushed her sister with one more question.

"Then shit, can I come with you? I want to have some fun too."

"Girl, please. Your ass always get bored after thirty minutes and be ready to come home," shot Lisa, which was the truth. Nesha hated going out.

"Yeah, you got me on that one," said Nesha as they both laughed.

"Look, sis," said Lisa in a serious voice, "I love the new me right now. I feel better and look better. I'm done with all that other shit. Plus, my baby 'bout to bring his ass home. My life is on the right track for the first time in a long time, and it's you who opened my eyes, although it took you beating my ass."

They both burst out laughing from the last part.

"All right, Lisa, I feel what you saying. I trust you, sis. Go have your little fun," said Nesha, sounding like a parent.

"Thank you, Momma," replied Lisa, and that made them laugh again.

"Fuck you, bitch," said Nesha. "Let's smoke before you go."

"I can do that," Lisa said.

They spent the next twenty minutes talking and smoking.

"Let me get my ass outta here. I'll be back soon." Lisa got up and walked to the front door, where she stopped and said to Nesha, "And don't be trying to wait up for me."

"Bitch, I ain't losing no sleep waiting up for your stanky ass," said Nesha.

"Whateva," replied Lisa, and she stepped outside. In her car, she pulled out her phone and dialed her trick for the evening.

"Hey, you," he said when he answered.

"Meet me at our hotel in thirty minutes," she said, and she hung up the phone.

Junebug's little brother smiled as he put his phone in his pocket and headed for his car.

*** Tank, for the last few days, had been walking on eggshells, anticipating his release date. They put him on S-time, which meant he was fourteen days or less to walking up out of there. *This shit really about to happen*, thought Tank. I can't wait to run out these gates.

His thoughts were interrupted when Porsche walked to the table he was sitting at and said, "Hey, Tank," sounding just like a bitch.

Tank still didn't fuck with anyone on the yard, but over the last few months, especially since the kitchen incident, he would nod at Porsche as if to say, "What's up?" when they passed each other on the yard. Today Tank was feeling so good, he didn't trip on Porsche for crossing the boundary line and invading his space. "Yo," said Tank, looking around the dayroom to see who was watching him.

"Damn, a nigga go on S-time and then start speaking," said Porsche, and he laughed.

"Yeah, I'm almost out this bitch," said Tank with a smile.

"I hope you don't come back to this shit. Everybody don't get the chance to leave hell walking," said Porsche.

"I'm good on this. Muthafuckas will read my obituary before they read another bed card," shot Tank, being serious.

"I know that's right," said Porsche with two snaps, "but you take care, and although it was a rough start, it's been a pleasure to have met you."

"Yep, you take care too," said Tank as Porsche walked away. *Yeah, ya'll won't be seeing the Tank again*, he thought as he sat there, thinking of all the shit he had gone through leading up to this point. "I fucked over some niggas and crossed some lines that I can never go back to," he mumbled to himself. "But I had to do what I had to do." Tank got up from the table and grabbed his workout gloves and headed to the yard to hit the dip and pull-up bars. "Fuck them niggas and the side of the line they on," he said as he did a pull-up. "It's all about me."

***

Junebug sat on his bunk, looking at the wall with a blank stare. He was trying to come up with some kind of idea for a poem. "Think, Junebug," he said to himself. He got up off the bunk and began to pace the floor of his cell. He walked back and forth a few times and then sat at his desk, where his paper and pen were. He began to write.

## Time vs. Punishment

We all seem to confuse time as being punishment, but it's not. It's the things you are taken from, like those once-in-a-lifetime moments you will never get the chance to see—the reality of knowing your child or loved ones needed your protection but you couldn't be there; hearing that your wife or girlfriend has decided to move on with the next man; lying down at night, and all you can hear is your child's small soft voice in the back of your mind asking you that heartbreaking question of "Daddy, when you coming home?"; hearing a family member say that your mom or dad is no longer with us—or maybe it's just realizing that you no longer dictate what you can and can't do. These are my punishments. Time don't mean anything. It's here, been here, and will continue to be here when I'm dead and gone. Time goes on, and we can never go back to get what time has taken away. If I was only sentenced to one day in jail but during that one day, death took someone I loved, then the judge may as well give me one million days because in my heart and mind, I will be punished forever. I can do time in prison with my head held high, but sometimes it's the things that come with that time that have my body balled up in a knot on my bunk.

"Damn," said Junebug to himself, "this some real shit." He read the paper again and knew that he had just put his life's story on paper. "This ain't no fucking poem. This me talking to me," he said. He jumped up from the desk with the paper in his hand and walked to the toilet, where he tore the paper into small pieces and then flushed them. He stood there and watched until every bit of it was gone. He went to his bunk and lay down. Before long, his body was balled up in a knot, just like the poem said. "I love you, Lisa," he mumbled. "No matter what, Ima always love you."***

In his eighth day of S-time, Tank was called into the counselor's office and told that he wouldn't be needed for the case against Cdog because a plea deal had been done. The counselor thanked Tank for his decision to do the right thing and hoped he would continue on the right path once he got out.

Tank walked out of the office with mixed emotions clouding his mind. He was happy that he didn't have to get on the stand in front of all those people and snitch, but he was also upset that he was the reason why a nigga would be trapped in the system forever, a system to this day he hated. Even now, with having a snitch jacket, Tank hated the police.

To ease his mind, he kept reminding himself that Cdog would've told on him, which, deep inside, he knew was a lie, but that lie made him feel that he had made the right choice. Tank shook his head and said to himself, "Fuck all this emotional shit." He walked to the phone and called Lisa. "Hey, little momma, just needed to hear your voice."

"It's good to hear your voice too, but why you sound like that?" she asked.

"I just want this shit to be over with, that's all," Tank answered.

"Soon," she said, trying to say it in his voice, which made them both laugh.

"That's why I called your ass. You know how to raise a nigga's spirit," said Tank.

"Shit, I can't wait until I get the chance to make other shit raise on you," Lisa said in her sexy voice.

"You got it raising right now," said Tank, looking down at his hard-on.

"Is it still big?" Lisa asked, now rubbing on her pussy.

"I think this muthafucka grew," said Tank, and he laughed.

"Mmmm," said Lisa as she moved her thong to the side and stuck her finger in her already-wet pussy. "What you going to do with it when you come home?" she asked as her finger went in and out of her pussy.

"Ima put it in every hole you let me and slowly stroke you until you say stop," he said.

"No, baby, don't stop," she moaned as she thrust her fingers really quickly into her pussy. "Keep it right there, Tank," she said when she felt that nut about to come.

Tank held the phone to his ear and listened as Lisa played with her pussy.

"Oh shit, Tank!" she yelled. "I'm about to cum. Keep it right there." Lisa put one of her fingers in her ass as he fucked her pussy. "Ahhh, ahhh. I'm cumming, Tank. Ahhh, you made me cum. Oh shit, this feel good. Ahhh, ahhh, mmmm."

Tank's dick was as hard as a brick, and being a few days to the house meant he would have to wait for some relief.

"Damn, that was a good one, nigga," Lisa said after she was done.

"It sounded like it," said Tank, and he laughed.

"I needed that, baby," lied Lisa. "I can't wait for the real dick to be in me."

"You and me both," shot Tank.

The recording over the phone said they had one minute remaining on their call.

"I love you, big daddy," said Lisa in a low tone.

"I love you too," said Tank. "Now go get that ass in the shower."

"Fuck you, nigga."

"You just did," said Tank, and they both laughed.

"Whateva," said Lisa, still laughing.

"Talk to you later, girl." Tank hung up the phone and walked to his cell to be let in.

The female c/o in the tower was fanning herself and smiling at him as she opened his door.

\*\*\*

Cdog sat on his bunk a few days after taking the plea deal and rolled himself a fat-ass joint. He no longer cared about being caught smoking. He needed the shit to ease his mind. *I already got two life terms. Plus, I'm about to do a sixty-month SHU program, so they can kiss my ass. Fuck them and their rules*, thought Cdog as he lit the joint and took a nice long pull.

"Good looking out, Curt" he said while coughing. "This some bomb shit." Cdog let the weed take action over his mind and lay back to enjoy his high. Now with his mind and body being on relax mode, he decided to write a couple of letters. "Ima answer the boy Cooper's letter first," mumbled Cdog. Cooper had asked him the last time he wrote if Cdog respected the efforts of people trying to stop gang violence.

Cdog wrote,

> Salutation, my friend. Just wanted to take time and share my input on the question you had asked me about stopping gang violence. I hope I can give you the insight you want. As we both know, people have devoted countless dollars to rid our streets of gang violence, which only meant locking the so-called troublemakers behind bars. We all know that's neither working nor solving the problem. It's time that a real solution be placed into all communities, a solution that relates to how our youth think, which, in return, will give

the answer to why they do what they do. A person coming from the middle or upper class does not have the answers to our problems in the inner or lower-class cities. The answer can only come from where the problem is and/or started. How can a so-called expert at Yale or Duke tell me about something I'm living every day? They are basically telling me who I am without knowing who I am (yeah, picture that). Being in a gang isn't a bad culture. We just didn't use the word *gang*. We used the word *tribe*. It's the activities of the gang that make it bad. If there was a gang that didn't allow its members to go to jail but instead sent them off to college, how bad would that gang be then? Truthfully, in the eyes of many agencies, that gang would be a threat at the highest level because their members would be at the table with those who decide and make the rules. At some point, we need to regain control of our kids, not their bodies but their thoughts. The body goes where the mind tells it. If we don't teach our kids to stand for something, then just like us, they will fall for anything. I bet you saying, "Damn, he sound like my brother right now" (LMAO). You may be correct. My eyes and mind have been opened to so much these past few months, and it's due in a major way to you and the letters you let me read. I can't thank you enough for your friendship. Until next time, peace be with you.

Cdog filled out the envelope and stuck the letter in his cell door for pickup. "I'm done writing for now," he said out loud. "It's fucking off my high." Cdog laughed as he walked to his bunk. He grabbed the other half of his joint and lit it.

*** Nesha and Tonya sat in the living room, gossiping and smoking on a blunt while Nesha took a break from doing Tonya's hair.

"So, girl, you been at your momma's house since Popeye went to jail?" asked Nesha.

"Yeah, I told that nigga I couldn't do it anymore," Tonya answered.

"Shit, I'm not mad at you," said Nesha, smacking her lips. "I call my sister stupid all the time for running her ass up there to Tank. Let my nigga go to jail, and Ima be like, 'Naw, boo-boo. Don't call me call your momma.'"

Nesha's last comment made them both laugh as they high-fived each other.

"I don't know how Lisa do it, but I knew from the jump I couldn't. They got his ass for murder. Ain't no way Ima just put my like on hold out here and run for his ass," said Tonya. "I'll keep it real and send him some money or a package when he need it, but that's where I'm drawing the line. I'm not writing any letters. 'Not coming to visit you and don't want to hear you on the phone, begging and pleading me to do any of that shit, so don't call.'" Tonya hit the blunt.

"You better than me because I ain't sending a nigga nothing," Nesha said, being serious.

"Ima do that for Popeye because I do still love his ass, and based on the way he took care of me, I can't see the nigga starve."

"I can feel you on that, but me? I'm not sending a nigga nothing," Nesha said again. "So when do they go to court?"

"I don't even know," answered Tonya. "I'm not keeping up with that shit."

"Okay, calm that shit down. I'm just asking," shot Nesha, hearing the attitude in Tonya's voice. "I know one thang though. Ain't been no dead bodies around here since them two niggas went to jail." Nesha had one of her eyebrows raised.

"I don't know what to tell you about that," said Tonya, but she did know. She had eavesdropped on a few of Popeye and Hitman's conversations. She knew about Cartoon's murder two days after they did it. She wasn't 100 percent sure, but she thought she had overheard them talking about that church incident. Tonya knew Popeye was a killer, but he had never done shit in front of her.

"Hello? Earth to Tonya. Come in," said Nesha, snapping her fingers in Tonya's face.

"What?" asked Tonya.

"Bitch, I asked you three times if you was ready for me to finish your hair. You was in some kind of daze or something," said Nesha, grabbing the hair off the table.

"I didn't hear you, girl, but yeah, I'm ready," Tonya said as she relit the blunt they were smoking. "Where Lisa at? I haven't seen her since I been here."

"Out trying to get shit for Tank. He will be home in a few days," said Nesha.

"Damn, for real? I didn't know he was that short to the house," stated Tonya.

"Yep, sometime next week, he will have his big black ugly ass walking through that door," Nesha said, and they both laughed.

"I hope he don't let his cousin fill his head up with bullshit about me," said Tonya.

They spent the next three hours talking and smoking, with Nesha finishing Tonya's hair, which was about the time Lisa had come through the door.

"Hey, sis, what you buy me?" Nesha asked, looking at the bags in Lisa's hands.

"The same thing I bought you last time," shot Lisa.

"Oh, nothing then," Nesha said, and they laughed.

"Hey, Lisa," said Tonya.

"Hey," replied Lisa. "Whose business you bitches talking about now?"

"Yours, mine, and a few others," answered Tonya, which made them all laugh.

Lisa pulled out an already-rolled blunt and sat on the couch, where they talked and giggled for the next few hours.

*** Popeye and Hitman both sat in the courtroom, waiting on their arraignment in the superior court. With the evidence against them being so concrete, the DA wasted no time pushing the case forward. The municipal part of court went by so quickly, even their lawyers said they hadn't seen a murder case get bonded over that quickly.

The judge finally came from his chambers and took his seat on the bench. He shuffled some papers and then announced their case. "We are here for the defendants to enter a plea and set a trial date," said the judge. "Is there any other matter the court needs to be made aware of regarding this case?"

"Not at this time, Your Honor," said the DA.

"We have no issues," stated Popeye's and Hitman's lawyers.

"With nothing holding us up, how do the two defendants plea to the charges?" asked the judge, and once again, the lawyers spoke as one.

"Not guilty, Your Honor."

"Their plea has been entered and recorded, so let's set a trial date," said the judge.

The DA stood up and said, "If it pleases the court, the state will be ready 120 court days from today, if that's okay with the defendants' attorneys."

There was a slight pause in the courtroom. Then the judge spoke.

"I see no objection, so therefore, the trial date is set for November 10 of this year." The judge closed the folder while picking up another one.

Hitman and Popeye were escorted back to the holding tank, where they would wait for the bus to return to the county jail.

"I hope the nigga I seen earlier is downstairs when we get there," said Hitman, lying on the concrete bench.

"What nigga?" asked Popeye.

"The nigga I caught peeking at either me or you when we was in the county tank. He look like one of them boys," said Hitman.

"And, nigga, you just now saying something?" asked Popeye, getting pumped up.

"Man, it was too early to be beating a nigga's ass or having the one time spray a nigga up with that Mace," answered Hitman.

"Fuck all that," said Popeye. "When it comes to them niggas, it ain't never too early to eat."

They both burst out laughing.

"I hope his ass still here and didn't leave on one of those early trips," finished Popeye.

"You and me both," shot Hitman, "but until they come get us, I'm about to take me a nap."

"Handle your business, fool. Ima knock me some pushups down," replied Popeye.

After about two hours, the police opened up the tank door.

"Let's go. It's time to head downstairs," said an officer.

Popeye and Hitman were put on an elevator and taken to the holding tank located in the basement of the court building. As soon as the police let them into the tank and closed the door, they began to hunt for the dude Hitman was talking about.

"Do you see the nigga or what?" asked Popeye.

"Naw, I don't see him," Hitman answered, still looking around the tank.

"Man, fuck all that," said Popeye as he stood up on one of the benches. "Aye, excuse me in the tank!" he shouted, and everybody turned to look at him. "I'm Popeye from the Bottoms, and I'm looking for all enemies."

Nobody said a word as Popeye stood there.

"Since there's no enemies, continue as you were." Popeye stepped down off the bench, and all Hitman could do was laugh.

"Your ass is stupid," said Hitman, shaking his head.

That announcement became a part of every court date.

"I'm just letting these niggas know," said Popeye. "Ima hit this phone right quick and call that bitch Lisa."

"Yep, I'm posted," said Hitman. "Bottoms"

"Bottoms," said Popeye as he walked off. Popeye dialed Lisa's number, and after four rings, he heard her answer.

"What it do, my nigga?" asked Lisa after accepting the charges.

"Not too much, just at this fuckin' court building," answered Popeye.

"If I had known, I would've came," said Lisa.

"Man, shut the fuck up with all that bullshit," said Popeye, and they both laughed.

"All right, my nigga, you got me on that one," said Lisa. "Your bitch was over here a couple days ago, getting her hair done."

"Fuck that bitch. She on some other shit right now," shot Popeye.

"Oh, so it's trouble in paradise?" asked Lisa.

"I'm not about to have this conversation with you," replied Popeye. "What's up with my cousin?"

"Home in a couple more days. I got him a cellphone already, so write his number down," said Lisa.

Popeye pulled out his pencil and wrote the number on his court paper.

"Call him in three or four days"

"Damn, he that short?" asked Popeye.

"Yep. Where Hitman at?'"

"He right here," answered Popeye. "Hold on." He motioned Hitman over and handed him the phone.

"Hello," said Hitman.

"What's up, fine-ass nigga?" asked Lisa in a sexy voice.

"Just one day at a time," he answered, blushing.

"So a bitch might not ever get some of that dick? You should've stop playing and got some of this bomb pussy," said Lisa.

"Damn, bitch. Ain't your man on his way home?" asked Hitman.

"Yeah, he is, nigga. What that got to do with what we could've done?" she asked.

Hitman shook his head as if to say, "This bitch crazy." "Aye, they just opened the door to take us back to the county. Popeye said he will holla at you later," shot Hitman.

"Okay. I got a few dollars for ya'll," said Lisa.

"Fo' sho'," said Hitman. "Bottoms."

"It'll be on ya'll books today, nigga. Bottoms," Lisa said back, and they both hung up the phone.

"Now that's a thirsty-ass bitch," said Hitman to Popeye.

"What you expect when she come from the Bottoms, nigga?" asked Popeye, and they both laughed, throwing up the Bottoms gang sign.

The police called their names for the bus headed back to the county jail.

*** Tank woke up feeling good. He knew that today was his last day of this prison shit. "I'm gone tomorrow," he said to himself as he looked in the mirror and shaved. *Just gotta get through one more day,* thought Tank. *I don't want ya'll breakfast, lunch, or dinner today.* "I'm gone!" Tank yelled, and he started doing a dance in the middle of the cell. He felt so good, he wanted to cry, so he did. Tears ran down his face as he smiled and did his dance. "Man, I'm really about to be out this bitch," he mumbled, looking around the small cell. "I ain't never coming back to this."

Tank cleaned his cell for what he called the last time ever. He looked at the bags of canteen he had pulled from under his bunk. *Who the fuck can I leave this with?* he asked himself. *Fuck it. Ima give it all to the punk Porsche. He did look out for me on that write-up.* Tank sat the three bags by the door.

"If you want yard and dayroom, flash your light," said the tower cop over the mic.

"Yeah, I need to call Lisa so she can have her ass up here tomorrow," Tank said, flashing his cell light. When the door opened up, he put the bags on the tier, grabbed his phone book, and then stepped out of the cell. Tank walked up to Porsche's door with one of the bags. "Aye, top of the day," said Tank. "Ima leave my canteen to you."

Porsche stood at the door in shock with his hand over his heart. "Dang, Tank, I don't know what to say. I really thought you didn't like me."

"Actually, I don't, so go ahead and tie your dick back down between your legs," said Tank, and he laughed.

"No, you didn't," said Porsche, putting his hands on his hips with a smile on his face.

"Come grab this other shit in front of my door," said Tank, "and once again, let me say thank you."

"You don't have to thank me, Tank. I already told you I didn't like that nigga anyway."

"Oh, I'm not just thanking you for that. I'm also thanking you for keeping all the homosexuals away from me so I didn't have to kill one of them muthafuckas," said Tank in a serious voice.

"Tank, we ain't bad people. We just gay."

"Whateva. Just come get the rest of this shit," said Tank, and he walked back to his cell door.

Porsche picked the two bags up when he had made it to Tank's cell. He turned and looked Tank in the eye and then, in a deep voice, said, "You take care, brah, and by the way, my real name is Vincent."

Tank shook his head and laughed all the way to the phone. He dialed Lisa's number.

"Hello," she said, half asleep.

"Wake your ass up, nigga," said Tank, and he laughed.

"I am up, baby," she lied as she lay in bed with her eyes closed.

"Look, I need you up here tomorrow at 7:00 a.m. to pick me up."

Lisa's eyes flew open, and she sat up in bed. "For real, Tank?" she asked excitedly, now all the way out of bed. "Don't fucking play with me."

"Naw, fo' real, fo' real," said Tank.

"Nigga, you just made me cum on myself," said Lisa, walking toward the bathroom.

"Just have your ass up here and wear a nice little skirt so I can play with that pussy on the way home."

"I'll be there and with no panties on," she replied with a giggle.

"Yep, lil momma, this nightmare about to end," said Tank.

"You just made my day, Tank. I can't wait for tomorrow. Damn, my baby coming home."

"So I'll see you then, baby," Tank told her.

"You sure will," she replied as they ended their call.

Lisa was in front of the prison the next morning at five thirty, parked and drinking coffee. She saw a van pull out of the prison gate at around eight o'clock. The van came to a stop, and a c/o jumped out of the passenger seat and opened the middle door of the van. A white inmate got out and went to the woman standing by her car. Lisa watched them hug and kiss. Lisa got out of the car and waved at the c/o, who looked back at her and then turned to the van and said something that she couldn't hear, but then she saw Tank, and her heart skipped a couple of beats. He climbed out of the van and started walking toward her, but she took off running to him and jumped into his arms when she reached him.

With tears of joy flowing down her face, she kissed Tank and said over and over, "Daddy's home. Daddy's home."

Tank and Lisa spent the first few days of his freedom fucking. Tank woke up in the pussy and went to sleep in the pussy. He did anything and everything he could think of to Lisa's pussy, and she took it like a champ. The more he drove his dick inside her, the harder she threw her pussy at him. On one of their lovemaking days, Lisa was sucking Tank's dick like she was trying to make it spit liquid gold.

Tank just lay back and enjoyed her mouth service. *This is the moment I've been waiting for*, thought Tank as he reached for the cellphone Lisa had given him the day he came home. He went to camera mode and began taking picture after picture of Lisa sucking his dick. She was so caught up in her sucking, she didn't notice, or maybe she just didn't care because in a few photos, she was looking right into the camera. *Yeah*, thought Tank. *Wait until that nigga see these.* He took a few more shots, put the phone down, and had Lisa ride his dick until they both cummed.

The next day, Tank walked into a photo store. He had them download and print the pictures. The dude behind the counter smiled at the images on his computer.

"You like that?" asked Tank, catching the dude looking.

"No, sir," answered the clerk. "What size would you like?"

"All five by seven," said Tank.

The clerk did as requested and handed Tank his copies.

After paying for the pictures, Tank looked the clerk in the eye and said with a smile, "I hope I don't see these on the internet."

Tank walked out of the store and went straight to the post office, where he pulled the already-filled-out envelope from the glove compartment. Tank placed ten photos inside and sealed it. He paid for next-day delivery.

"I want you to get these as fast as possible, my boy," Tank said to himself. "Oh yeah, I can't wait for your reply."

*** "I got some mail for you," said the c/o standing at Junebug's cell door.

"Oh yeah? It ain't no prison mail, is it?" asked Junebug, walking to the door.

"Naw, it's from the outside, and there's some pictures," said the c/o.

*Must be from my little bro*, thought Junebug as he reached for the envelope. When he saw the address, his heart stopped beating for a while, it seemed. *Damn, Lisa finally came to her senses*, thought Junebug. He walked to his bunk, and his body was shaking like an old mini bike. *I got my Lisa back*. He began to remove the tape the prison mail room had put on the envelope. The front had a prison stamp saying, "No letter, ten photos only."

Junebug began pulling the pictures out and couldn't believe what he was seeing. *I can't believe Lisa did this to me*, thought Junebug as he looked at the photos. They were pictures of her and Tank fucking and of her sucking Tank's dick. There was even a photo of Tank looking at the camera, smiling.

"Why, Lisa?" Junebug asked out loud. "Do you really hate me this much? I love you." He began crying. He looked at the photos for what he said would be the last time, but for some reason, he wasn't able to take his eyes away from the pictures. Even when snot and tears fell on them, he continued to look. *I should've got that nigga Tank when I saw him*, thought Junebug. "You hurt me, Lisa," he said while still crying. "I have nothing to live for." Junebug raised his eyes from the photos and took a look around his cell. "Y'all will be sorry for this! *Fuck the world!*"

He grabbed the sheet off his bunk and began twisting it until it became ropelike. He then wrapped it around the light in his cell while sitting on the top bunk. Once he thought it was tight and strong enough to hold his weight and short enough to keep his feet from touching the floor, he put it into a noose, which he slid over his head and around his neck. He pulled the noose tight until he began to choke.

"*Fuck all ya'll!*" he screamed one last time before jumping off the top bunk and snapping his neck in two places.

Junebug had a second of regret, but his hands just wouldn't move, and his body began to feel numb. He closed his eyes while hanging from the light and asked God to please remove him from this life, inside this hell he was confined in. He opened up his eyes for the last time and looked down at the bottom bunk. All he could see was Lisa sucking Tank's dick in the photo. Then everything went black.

\*\*\* Popeye and Hitman stood by their cell door, waiting to go out for roof time.

"I need some of this fresh air," said Hitman.

"Yeah, me too," replied Popeye. "We been stuck in this building for the last two weeks."

"Roof time, roof time," said the police over the loudspeaker as the door began to open.

They stepped out onto the tier and did their ritual of looking both ways and letting everyone walk past them before they fell in line.

"Ima hit that number Lisa gave me on Tank and see if that fool made it home yet," said Popeye.

"Tell that nigga I said Bottoms. He might not remember me. It's been so long," said Hitman.

They reached the roof, and Popeye went toward the phones, while Hitman made his way to the vending machines. Popeye dialed the number and listened as the phone rang.

Tank answered and then accepted the call. "Hello," said Tank.

"Cuzzo," replied Popeye, getting happy. "You home."

"Yeah, they freed me, my boy, but what's the deal with you?" asked Tank.

"Man, you already know. You just left this shit. They pushing hard against us right now," answered Popeye.

"Just keep fighting, nigga. They gon' get tired and drop their guards and what when they start throwing niggas deals," said Tank.

"Yep, but look, cuzzo, I'm glad you touched back down on them streets. This shit ain't looking good for me."

"It ain't over 'til it's over, nigga, so just keep hope on your mind. Shit, look at me. I came from under my shit," said Tank, trying to lift his cousin up.

"Nigga, hope is hard to believe in when you got these white folks licking their chops. They really pressing hard on our case," said Popeye.

"What's the deal with Hitman?" asked Tank.

"As solid as they come," answered Popeye.

"Fo' sho', fo' sho', so Tonya ain't doing nothing for you?" asked Tank.

"Naw, she all fucked up in the head right now. She back at her momma's house, and I can't even call there."

"Well, I'm here, my nigga. Ima keep some money on the phone so you can hit me whenever," said Tank.

"I got a few dollars put up, and I had plans to hit you with some of it when you came home," stated Popeye.

"All bullshit to the side, I could use some help right now. Shit, I don't even have my own car yet," replied Tank.

"My car just sitting up at my mom's house, so go ahead and snatch it. That's yours," said Popeye.

"Man, that ain't nothing but love," said Tank.

"But trip, I got the money buried at my old spot that me and Tonya had. I didn't get the chance to let her know where it was before she started acting crazy. All you gotta do is go to the water hose and pull it to its full length to the left of the hose. Start digging. It's right there," said Popeye.

"What you want me to do? Get you a lawyer?" asked Tank.

"Shit, with the evidence they got against us, that would be a waste of money. Just hold my part, and I'll let you know what to do with it," said Popeye.

"How much we talking?" asked Tank.

"Almost two hundred racks," answered Popeye.

Tank's mind went into overdrive when he heard the amount. *I love you, cuzzo, but you about to take another loss,* thought Tank with greed. "Oh, you was out here making a few moves while I was gone, huh?" asked Tank.

"Naw, not like that. I was able to stumble upon a dollar here and there," replied Popeye.

"Give me a day or two, and I'll swing by there to grab it. Call me back then," said Tank.

"No doubt. I'm glad you home, my boy. I can't trust nobody else. I'll hit you in a few days. I love you, fool," said Popeye.

"I love you too," said Tank, and he hung up the phone.

Tank walked to Lisa's car and drove straight to Popeye's old house. No one had moved in yet. He did exactly what Popeye had said with the water hose and started digging. *"Jackpot!"* he yelled as he pulled up the clear plastic bag full of money.

Popeye called him back.

The phone rang once and then went to a recording. "The number you have dialed is no longer in service."

*I must've hit the wrong number,* thought Popeye as he redialed.

The same recording was played.

"What the fuck?" Popeye said to himself. He knew Lisa's number had been the same for years, so he dialed her number, but once again, the same recording played. "Naw, cuzzo, don't do me like this." Popeye slammed the receiver down, knowing that he had just got worked by his cousin.

\*\*\* Cdog couldn't believe the letter he was reading from his sister, Karen. She told him that Tank was out, and from what she had heard, he was back doing the same shit he was doing before he had left. He had been out for about a month, just laid up at Lisa's house. Then she went on in her letter to say that someone told her Junebug had killed himself in his cell and that the police had found pictures laid out on his bunk of Lisa sucking on Tank's dick, which they were saying was the reason he had hanged himself. *Damn*, thought Cdog. *Junebug was a good nigga. I hope that's just a rumor, but how the fuck that nigga Tank get outta here? He must've been telling for a while. I know they didn't let him go just for my case.*

Cdog's mind went into overdrive, thinking about how he needed to get word out to the Bottoms to let niggas know that Tank was no good. *I don't have the paperwork on him yet, and that may be a problem. The only nigga who would've knocked him down just based on my word was Big Cdog, and he resting in peace. I need to have Karen holla at the general. Cbone will know how to handle this situation, but then again, without paperwork, he might not want to get involved.*

"Fuck!" yelled Cdog. He began to pace his cell, trying to come up with a solution. *That nigga Tank is poison, and everything he touch gon' go bad.* "Why didn't I listen to Junebug?" he asked himself as he walked. "Junebug straight knew." *That nigga Cooper need to send me a copy of my case. Then no one will have an excuse on why they didn't handle their business on Tank. That nigga need to die in a slow, painful way. Fuck blowing his brains out. That's too quick,* thought Cdog. *His death need to be spread out for some days.*

"I wish I could put my hands on you," Cdog mumbled. "Fuck, I wish I could put my hands on you." Then he dropped to the floor and did the only thing that cleared his mind, pushups, and he went hard on them. He usually did twenty-five hundred throughout the day, but he did that and some within an hour, taking minor breaks. "If I ever get my hands on you, Tank, Ima snap every bone in your body one by one," Cdog said with a smile.

\*\*\* For the life of her, Lisa couldn't understand why Junebug had done that to himself and why his momma blamed her for everything. *That old bitch looked like she was ready to gun me down in the grocery store when I saw her,* thought Lisa. *Shit, I haven't messed with Junebug for the last seven years, so how they gon' blame me? Oh, well. They can think what they want and point their finger at me, but in reality, they know what the fuck it is. That nigga* *was tripping. Yeah. Tank ass did some foul shit by sending those pictures. All I did was let Tank read the letter Junebug sent me. Then his momma had the nerve to say I helped take my daughter's father away,* thought Lisa as she replayed the conversation from the store in her head.

"No, my daughter's father been dead! He ain't done shit for her!" Lisa had yelled at Junebug's momma. "And from this day on, you don't have to worry about seeing my baby again!"

*I'm not fucking playing. They won't ever see her. She won't even be at his funeral.*

"Hey, baby," said Tank, interrupting her thoughts.

"Hey," she said back with no emotion in her voice.

"So you mad at me, huh?" asked Tank. "I didn't think the nigga would kill himself."

"You just don't fucking get it, do you, Tank?" she asked, now getting mad. "You used me as a pawn in your bullshit game."

"I didn't use you, Lisa," lied Tank. "I just wanted to hurt that nigga bad, and the only way I seen to do that was to feed or attack his obsession over you."

"Well, thank you for involving me in your plot, Tank," shot Lisa. "I thought shit was gon' be different for us when you got out, but it's the same old shit. You even got me changing my phone number. What's next, Tank?"

"Shit is different, Lisa, and Ima do whatever it takes to show you."

Lisa looked up into Tank's eyes and decided at that point, she would stand by her man. "No more kid games?" she asked.

"I promise," Tank shot back. "How about we play some grown-up games?" he asked while taking off his shirt.

"Mmmm, I like the sound of that," said Lisa in a sexy voice, "but, nigga, don't even think about taking a picture."

They both laughed and then spent the next two hours sucking and fucking.

***

"What's the deal, my boy?" asked Hitman. "You been walking around the last few days looking like you want to kill something."

"My bad, man," replied Popeye, lying on his bunk. "It's that nigga Tank."

"Y'all done fell out already? Don't tell me it's behind that bitch Lisa," said Hitman.

"Shit, I wish it was behind that rat-ass bitch," answered Popeye. Then he ran down the situation to Hitman. "Both of their phones are off now, so I can't contact them."

"I know that's your family, but how the fuck you trust him with that much money and your car?" asked Hitman.

All Popeye could do was shake his head as he thought about the situation. "Yeah, that nigga played my ass," said Popeye.

"Naw, you played yourself," shot Hitman, being honest. "See, that's why I got my money at five different spots. A muthafucka ain't gon' get me for all mine."

"Okay, smart-ass nigga, you win the award for spreading you money out," said Popeye, starting to get mad.

"Nigga, I don't need no fucking award for shit I do. Don't get mad at me. I'm not the nigga spending your money," said Hitman, now mad himself.

"Naw, Hitman, I'm not mad at you, and that's my bad for lashing out at you," said Popeye. "I just can't believe Tank did that shit to me."

"It seem like it's always our family that fuck over us," said Hitman. "I got you, my nigga, on some bread, but what you gon' do about Tank?"

"Really, ain't shit I can do right now, not from here, at least," answered Popeye.

"Well, like I said before, ya'll are family, and you gon' deal with him the way you see fit, but know this, my boy. In my eyes, me and you are family, so it's gon' be what it's gon' be if I run into him," said Hitman.

\*\*\* Cdog had just finished his workout and was getting his stuff ready for his birdbath when his left eye began to jump.

All his life, his mom had always said, "If your left eye jump, then somebody going to make you mad, so to stop whoever or whatever that's on the way, you gotta stick your finger in your mouth and then use that finger to make the cross sign over your left eye."

*And don't get her started about the right eye or when the palm of your hand itch*, thought Cdog with a smile on his face. Cdog filled the sink with water and then laid towels on the floor to keep the water from going out of the cell and onto the tier. *Jump, jump, jump, jump.* "Damn, my eye won't stop jumping," he said as he once again did the cross sign over it. He began his birdbath, and throughout it, his eye continued to jump. Cdog was finished with the bath and started cleaning up his cell when a c/o walked to his door.

"Aye, Johnson, what's your prison number?" the c/o asked, and after Cdog had told him the number, the c/o said, "I got some legal mail for you. Sign your name on this line." He pointed.

*Oh yeah*, thought Cdog, *this must be that paperwork from Cooper.*

"Open it up and wave the papers," said the c/o.

Cdog, without even looking at the front of the envelope, tore open the back and pulled out the papers. He waved them at the c/o and then put them back in the envelope and threw the letter on his bunk. Cdog went back to cleaning up the mess he had made from his birdbath. *Jump, jump, jump, jump.* His left eye was going crazy. After Cdog was done cleaning up the cell, he washed his dirty laundry.

"Ima take me a nap after all this," he said to himself. *Jump, jump, jump.* He made the cross sign once again. Cdog hung up his wet laundry and then walked to his bunk, where he picked up the envelope and, still without looking at it, tossed it on his desk and then lay down and closed his eyes. *Jump, jump, jump, jump.* Cdog rolled onto his side and went to sleep.

About two hours later, Cdog was jolted from his sleep by a c/o who was yelling down the tier, "Turn your lights on if you want chow!"

"Damn," said Cdog, "I must've been tired as fuck."

He got up from his bunk and went to the cell door. The c/o was three cells down from him, passing out dinner trays. Cdog turned on his light when they made it to him and got his tray. "I could've stayed asleep for this shit," he said out loud to himself while looking at the food. After eating the salad and cake, he set the tray by the door for pickup. Cdog washed his hands and then brushed his teeth. He went back to his bunk and took a seat. He reached over to the desk and grabbed the legal mail he had gotten earlier. "Yeah, Tank, I got the paperwork on your ass now," Cdog said as he pulled out the contents of the envelope.

From the first glance, he knew the mail didn't come from Cooper. "This from the appeal courts," mumbled Cdog as he began to read what they had sent him. The first part of their brief was them giving a summary of his case, and it all sounded bad until Cdog got to the last few pages, where it stated that they, the Federal Court, had reversed the lower state courts' findings with extreme prejudice and exonerated Curtis Johnson from any and all prosecution regarding this matter. "The sentence of life in prison is hereby taken away, and if there's no other pending matters against Curtis Johnson, then he shall be released from the custody of the department of corrections forthwith."

Cdog couldn't believe what he had just read, so he read it again. Then he read it again. *They overturned my original case,* thought Cdog. Then reality slapped the shit out of him. "I could've went home," he said, now thinking about the life sentence he took for the c/o's murder. Cdog began to shake as he rocked back and forth on his bunk. Then all at once, no longer being able to contain it, he began to cry, not a normal "I'm angry" cry but an "I lost everything" cry. Snot and slobber ran down his face with the tears and fell onto his chest. "Oh god, this hurt," he said out loud as he cried.

*Jump, jump, jump* went his left eye, and he knew his momma was right with her saying. Cdog felt like nothing mattered except balling up on his bunk and crying. He cried until tears no longer came out of his eyes, and for the next four days, all Cdog did was lie on his bunk and cry. He didn't eat. He didn't shit. He didn't work out, which he loved doing. He just lay there and cried on his piss-filled mattress. It took him four long days to stop the crying, but his body and mind were still in so much pain. "Why? Why did I go down this path?" Cdog mumbled. He lay on his bunk and just stared at the top bunk as if it was a movie screen. All the things he had been through up to now seemed to be flashing by—Hotdog's murder, the c/o's murder, Tank walking out the back door, him taking the plea deal, the letter from the courts. These things rolled by like a silent movie to him as he looked at the bunk.

*** Lisa and Tank's relationship was on rocky grounds. It seemed to Lisa that ever since Popeye had given Tank that car, the nigga couldn't sit still. He had even claimed to be spending nights at his momma's house. Now here it was. The nigga hadn't answered his phone in two days.

"What the fuck, Tank? I been calling and leaving messages, but you haven't gotten back. So, baby, can you please call me ASAP? I love you," Lisa said on Tank's answering machine.

She got up and got dressed and then headed out the door. *I'm not about to be just sitting here, stressing over that nigga,* thought Lisa. *I got shit I can be doing myself.* She turned her car uptown, where the rich people lived, and pulled into a hotel parking lot twenty minutes later. Lisa grabbed her phone and dialed a number. "I'm here" was all she said. Then she hung up the phone.

*** Tank had been feeling a little sick the last few days, and he had noticed that since being home, he was losing weight at a rapid pace. *I must've* *caught one of those bugs that's been going around*, he thought. *If I don't feel any better by tomorrow, Ima take my ass to the hospital.*

The next day, Tank woke up feeling worse than the day before, so he showered, got dressed, and drove straight to the emergency room. He filled out the papers required to see the doctor and then took a seat and waited for his name to be called. After twenty minutes of screaming kids running around the waiting room, Tank became irritated and walked outside. As soon as his nose caught a smell of fresh air, it made him vomit. He vomited green and yellow stuff until nothing else came out except the sound of throwing up.

Tank ran back into the hospital and went to the nurse he had given his papers to. "I need to see the doctor now," Tank told her and tried to walk to the back.

"Sir, I need you to go take a seat and wait on your turn," said the nurse.

That was when Tank fainted. The nurse yelled out a code, and two doctors appeared from nowhere. They ordered the nurse to have Tank taken to observation, where they stuck him with an IV and took blood for tests.

When Tank finally woke up, he was hooked to three different machines. He took a look around the room, trying to figure out what was going on. Then it hit him. "Oh yeah, I drove myself here" he said to himself.

"So you woke up, huh?" asked the nurse when she came into the room. "I need to check your vitals."

Tank watched as she went about doing her job. When she finished, Tank asked how long he would be there.

"That's up to the doctor," answered the nurse.

"Then when will I see him? Tank asked.

"He should be making his rounds within the hour," she said. "Do you need water or anything?"

"Naw, I'm good. I just want to know what's wrong with me."

"You will have to talk to the doctor about that," said the nurse, and she walked out of the room.

Tank lay in the hospital bed, watching TV for what seemed like forever, before the doctor came in.

"Hello, Mr. Robinson. How are you feeling right now?" the doctor asked.

"Right now, I feel all right," replied Tank. Then he told the doctor everything, from feeling sick to vomiting in front of the hospital and fainting. "My vomit was some green and yellow stuff."

"And weight loss has been a concern also?" asked the doctor.

"Yeah," Tank answered.

"We took some blood while you were asleep, and I'm having tests done, but by law, I have to ask if it's okay to test for AIDS and HIV."

"HIV?" said Tank "You think I got AIDS?"

"It's only a precaution, and like I said, by law, I have to get you permission. So it's okay to do it?" asked the doctor.

"Yeah, it's cool. When can I get outta here?"

"There's no reason to keep you if you feel better. Plus, we have all your contact info, so as soon as we hear something, we will let you know."

"How long is the wait on these tests?" Tank asked.

"We should know something by next week," he told Tank. "Until then, try to get some rest." The doctor walked out of the room.

That was when Tank jumped up from the bed, snatching the needles and tubes out of his arms. He went to the closet and got his clothes.

After four long weeks, Tank received the phone call that changed his life forever, and he vowed to make the one person responsible for it pay with their life.

*** Cdog sat in classification and wasn't even paying attention to what they were saying.

"After being found guilty of the A1 offense, we will be going with the CC2 recommendation for a sixty-month SHU, 365 days' loss of credit, and one year of C-over-C status. Do you have any questions, Mr. Johnson?" asked the warden.

"Naw," answered Cdog. "I'm just ready to get the fuck away from this prison."

"Watch your language," said the captain.

"How 'bout you watch my ass walk outta here? Because I don't give a fuck about nothing ya'll talking about," shot Cdog.

The c/o dug his fingers into Cdog's shoulder, but all Cdog did was look up at him.

"Inmates like you are the reason why we have SHU buildings," said the warden with a smirk, "and I hope they make you spend every single day of the sixty months back there. I wish we could give you more."

Cdog let out a loud laugh as he looked the warden in the eye. "This little bullshit power you think you have don't mean shit to me. None of ya'll in this room can do anything that would mean more than the life sentence I have, so fuck that sixty-month SHU. Ima be in jail anyway regardless of where I do it at."

"Get his ass outta here," said the captain to the c/os, who snatched Cdog up by the collar on his jumpsuit and began dragging him toward the door.

"Fuck ya'll!" screamed Cdog. "Take these cuffs off me and see what I do!"

"Shut the fuck up," said a c/o, and then he hit Cdog on his chin as they made it out of the sight of the warden.

"*You a straight bitch!*" shouted Cdog to the c/o who had hit him. "You better hope I never get the chance 'cause Ima do you like I did the last one!"

Cdog felt another blow to the back of his head as the c/os dragged him back to his cell. They threw him, unconscious, to the floor, and the tower officer closed the cell door. The c/os didn't even bother to take the cuffs off.

Twelve days later, Cdog was taken to the SHU and was only two cells down from where Junebug had killed himself.

*** After only one hour of deliberation, Popeye and Hitman were brought back into the courtroom.

"Have, Your Honor," said the jury foreman.

*Damn,* thought Popeye as he looked around the court. *They pushed hard and fast on our case. They only put two witnesses on the stand, and both of them claimed to be gang experts. Ross was one of them. That fucking video is what sealed their case.*

"The clerk will now read the verdict," said the judge.

"We, the jury, find the defendants in court, on murder, guilty," read the clerk.

Popeye's lawyer asked that the jury be polled, so the judge went one by one, and each juror stood and stated, "Guilty."

The judge thanked the jury for their service and then dismissed them. "We will set the date for sentencing thirty days from today," said the judge.

"We are formally announcing our motion for appeal, Your Honor," said Popeye's lawyer.

"Have your motion written and submitted by the sentence date, and if there're no other matters, then this case is over," announced the judge.

"There're no other matters, Your Honor," said the DA.

Just like that, Popeye and Hitman were ushered out of the courtroom. They both sat in the holding tank, quiet and in deep thought, wondering what life had in store for them in prison.

"Man, we gon' die in prison. They ain't gon' never let us out" said Hitman. Popeye looked at his homie and realized what he had just said was the truth. Their feet would never touch the ground of the hood they called Bottoms again. *Damn*, thought Popeye. Then the voice of Officer Ross came to his mind. "So you just going to leave that pretty girl out here." Popeye just shook his head.

Thirty days later, Popeye and Hitman were back at the defense table, facing the judge.

"We are here today for sentencing and for the motion of appeal to be filed. Are there any other matters?" asked the judge, but no one in the courtroom said a word. "Okay then. We will proceed." The judge then handed down life-without-parole sentences to both Popeye and Hitman like he was passing out lunch.

"Men like you two," he said, pointing, "are the reason why there's so much evil in the world."

"Can we get the fuck up outta here? You already gave us our time. Fuck you, your speech, and the world you talking about," said Hitman.

"Bailiff, get both of them out of my courtroom," said the judge, mad as hell.

The last thing they heard was the judge saying something about sending them forthwith. Three weeks later, they arrived at the prison reception center.

\*\*\* "I knew it. I knew it," said Tank, hitting the steering wheel of his car while sitting in the liquor store parking lot, where he had just purchased two half gallons of gin.

*I knew something was wrong*, thought Tank as he took a long swallow from one of the bottles. *I been losing weight and feel fucked up all the time. That's why I had to make that hospital trip a few weeks ago. Then today the doctor called me and told me I have full-blown AIDS.* Tank took another drink. *This shit had to come from that bitch Lisa. She the only one I been fucking since I came home.* He took another drink. *That bitch gave me this shit from day one. Damn. What was I thinking? I knew better than to trust her rat ass.* Tank started the car and pulled off. *I'm going right to her house and blow her face off if she can't tell me something.* "Tell me what?" Tank said to himself. "The doctor already told me the deal." *Ima just kill that bitch.*

He turned onto Lisa's street. "Yeah, the bitch at home," he said, looking at her car in the driveway. After parking, he took a long hard swallow of gin and then reached under his seat for the .357 Python. He jumped out of the car after checking and concealing the gun and walked toward her house. The door opened up just as he got to it, and Lisa greeted him.

"Hey, baby, you sure here early."

"Yeah, I didn't have shit else to do, so I came this way," Tank lied.

"Well, I'm glad you did," Lisa said in a sexy voice.

"Oh, so we alone?" Tank asked.

"Yep, just you and me. Have you been drinking? I smell liquor," said Lisa.

"I had a little sip," Tank said as he stepped inside the house.

Lisa closed the door behind him, and when she spun around to face Tank, the Python was damn near touching her nose. "What the fuck, Tank?" Lisa asked, and she tried to move the gun.

"Bitch, you killed me, so Ima kill you," replied Tank. Then he pulled the trigger.

He watched as Lisa's head flew back from the impact of the bullet. Her body went limp and hit the floor. Tank put the nozzle of the gun against her chest, where her heart was, and pulled the trigger again, this time certain she was dead. "Go join your baby daddy, you worthless, rat-ass bitch," Tank said to Lisa's body.

He put the gun back up and opened the front door. Seeing no one, he stumbled to his car. He sat in Lisa's driveway, drinking. He finished off the first bottle without even breaking a sweat, but when he made it halfway into the second bottle, his mind started telling him that he needed to get out of there.

He started his car, and at first, he felt he could drive, but once he backed out of the driveway and put the car in drive, his foot smashed down on the gas pedal like a ton of bricks. Tank went flying down the small street, reaching speeds of eighty-five miles per hour. He shot through the first stop sign with no problem. On the next stop sign, he barely missed hitting a truck, but he kept his foot pressed on the pedal.

Tank saw the next stop sign, but for some off reason, he sped up, and just as the front of his car hit the crosswalk, he saw a Corvette pulling out from the opposite direction. Tank, unable to do anything, T-boned the Corvette, sending the female passenger flying through the windshield and slamming headfirst into a parked car, snapping her neck. The male driver of the Corvette never stood a chance either as the steering wheel came off, and his chest slammed against the pole, puncturing his heart as the pole came out of his back.

Tank couldn't feel his legs and knew the police would be on their way. He put the bottle of gin to his lips and drank it until there was no more. He looked out to the crowd that had started to gather. He watched as one of his little homies came to his car and asked if he was all right. Tank smiled at him and then pulled the gun out. The young dude ran from the car. Tank looked around one last time before he put the gun to his head and, with a smile on his face, blew his brains out.

The couple that he had T-boned and killed were Lil Cdog's parents.

*** Four years and five months into his five-year SHU term, Cdog stood at his cell door, feeling defeated inside, although he had become one of the biggest dudes in the prison system from constant workout routines that resulted into rock-hard twenty-four-inch arms, coupled with the mind of a genius from reading whatever he got his hands on. He was able to complete three college courses and taught himself how to speak Spanish and Swahili while in the SHU, but he had lost everything he held dear to his heart: his freedom for the rest of his life, both his parents, and two homies whom he loved as brothers. The only purpose for his heart now was to beat and pump blood through his body. Love had been removed from it, and he wasn't sure if it, *love*, would ever return. The only feeling that kept him getting up from bed to face his day was revenge.

He had heard that Popeye was in prison with life for the murder of Cartoon. Cdog couldn't wait for the confrontation between him and Popeye. He had already cemented the idea in his head and decided that it was just one of those things that needed to be done regardless of the consequences. *Man, if I had just listened to Junebug,* Cdog thought for the last few years, *none of this shit would've happened. You told me Tank was no good, and for not believing you, I feel responsible for your death.* "That bitch-ass nigga Tank," mumbled Cdog as he came back to the present day. "You took everything from me, and I can't even make you pay for it."

Cdog continued to stand at his cell door and stared out at nothing. He didn't see the other cells, the stairs, the shower, or the few benches in his pod. All he saw was empty space at that moment.

"No mail for you today, Johnson," said the c/o, who seemed to pop out of the sky.

"What?" asked Cdog, blinking really quickly.

"I said no mail. What, you was in another world or something?" the c/o asked.

"Naw, man. Just daydreaming, I guess," replied Cdog.

"Are you all right?" asked the c/o, who knew about Cdog's situation with the death of his parents.

"Yeah, I'm good," answered Cdog. "I'm just waiting on my moment."

The c/o looked at Cdog for a minute with concern. "Okay," said the c/o as he walked off toward the next cell.

Cdog turned from the door and went to the floor in the pushup position. "Just waiting on my moment as I'm doing life in hell," Cdog said to himself as he began his workout for the third time that day. *I hope they ready for me 'cause I'm coming. On Bottoms."*

## Book One Ends

Lightning Source UK Ltd.
Milton Keynes UK
UKHW041041070220
358341UK00001B/31/J